Birdie's Bargain

Birdie's Bargain

KATHERINE PATERSON

CANDLEWICK PRESS

Copyright © 2021 by Minna Murra, Inc.

First edition 2021

Library of Congress Catalog Card Number 2021945666
ISBN 978-1-5362-1559-5

21 22 23 24 25 26 LBM 10 9 8 7 6 5 4 3 2 1

Printed in Melrose Park, IL, USA

This book was typeset in ITC Esprit.

Candlewick Press
99 Dover Street
Somerville, Massachusetts 02144

www.candlewick.com

This book is for

Susan Cohen,
who loved the little nestling,
and

Karen Lotz,
who gently nudged the fledgling
to the edge of the nest,
and

you, her reader,
without whom she cannot fly.

If you're wearing a T-shirt that says in big capital letters **I ♥ JESUS**, you shouldn't be standing in the middle of the street bawling your eyes out. But that was exactly what Birdie was doing. She had raced out of Gran's house just in time to see the old Subaru swing around the corner. Mom must have been driving because Birdie got a last glimpse of Daddy sitting next to Baby Billy's car seat. They never looked back, and they didn't hear her yelling, telling them to wait—that she had changed her mind—that she wanted to go with them.

It was too late.

1
The Time of No Goodbyes

It wasn't until the volunteers from the Lions Club had left and they stood in the empty apartment looking at nothing that Birdie realized her bicycle was gone. The sofa, the kitchen table and chairs, all the beds—even the TV—had been carried to the truck. Daddy had finished stuffing the trunk of the Subaru and the tiny U-Haul trailer with all the boxes and baby furniture when she thought of it.

"Mom! Those guys stole my bike!"

"Oh, Birdie. No one stole your bike."

"Then where is it? Daddy didn't put it in the car or in the U-Haul. You gotta call them. Tell them to bring it back! Now!"

"We can't do that, sweetie." Mom sighed. She'd been doing a lot of sighing lately, and it wasn't her style. "I'm sorry. I should have told you, but it's been hard to think straight, and they were so thrilled to get a bike. They said bikes always do well in their summer sale."

"But it's *my bike*!"

"There was just no room, either in the car or the U-Haul . . . Did you know everything they make from the sale goes to help blind people?"

As if that would make it okay.

"It was really too small for you," Daddy chimed in. "We need to get you a new one, a regular-size one." He studied Birdie's grim expression. "I promise."

"When?"

"As soon as we can afford it," Mom said. Like never.

It was downhill from there. Birdie hardly spoke in the car on the way north even though Daddy was sitting in the back seat, too. The passenger-side front seat was piled to the roof with stuff, which meant that some grown-up had to sit in back. "Your mom's the better driver," he said as he climbed in with Birdie and Billy.

She was sure that before Billy was born, Daddy used

4

to drive a lot, and he never sat in the back even when he wasn't driving. She should have been happy he was in the back, but Baby Billy's car seat was plunk in the middle—right between them—and even if she felt like talking, which she certainly did not at the moment, how could she talk to Daddy across the stomach of a six-month-old baby who cried a lot and wouldn't even go to sleep in a moving car?

It was a known fact that every normal baby in the world just naturally passed out as soon as a car was shifted into drive and began to move. "I think something must be wrong with your brother," Melanie had said when Birdie complained to her friends that Billy never slept in the car.

During the whole week that Mom and Daddy and Gran tried to settle the family into their new quarters, Birdie watched soap operas. She hated the place, hardly bigger than a closet, that was supposed to be her new bedroom. She spent her days in the living room watching TV. They should have yelled at her for being lazy and selfish. They didn't even fuss at her for watching daytime soaps.

They just didn't care. Didn't they remember how they used to fuss about children turning into ignorant couch potatoes? Maybe she needed to scream like Billy so they'd come running. But seriously . . .

On Monday Mom had gone to the local Dollar Store and applied for a job. Daddy said she should take her time, try to find a better job, but she shook him off. They were hiring at the Dollar Store. She was sure she could get a job there. If she hated it, she'd try to find something else. Right now, they needed the money. She promised not to start before he left. No one suggested that Birdie start school before then.

They wanted as much time with Daddy as possible. But Birdie had pretty much ruined that, hadn't she? Moping around and pretending to feel sick for most of the week. Even Wednesday night, when Gran took them all out for maple creamies, Birdie had pouted. Chocolate was her favorite, not maple. Couldn't they bother to remember that?

Then the terrible last morning arrived. Mom came to wake her up, but Birdie just burrowed under the pillow and pretended to be asleep.

"Come on, sweetie. Get up." Birdie didn't move. "Birdie, please. We're not going to see Daddy for a year. Even if you don't want to go to the airport, at least get up and say goodbye."

"I can't." Her voice was muffled by the thick duck-feather pillow, to which she was probably allergic, but who would care? "I feel awful. I might give him something."

"Oh, Birdie," Mom said in her don't-be-ridiculous tone of voice. She stood in the doorway for a moment or two, then, sighing loudly enough for Birdie to hear it through the feathers, she left. Birdie listened to the click of her boot heels as she walked the short distance to the kitchen.

Birdie thought she could hear a whispered conversation, and then there was the sound of her father's heavier step. "Birdie." He said it quietly because he had walked right to the side of her bed. "I've got to go now, okay?"

What a stupid thing to say. It was not okay. It would never be okay.

"I want you to help your mom and Gran while I'm gone. No kidding, slugger. I really need you to step up to the plate." Why did he say that? She hated baseball.

7

When she didn't answer, didn't even turn to look at him, he bent down, gently pulled the pillow off her head, and kissed her ear. "I'll miss you, baby," he said. And was gone.

The closing of the heavy front door made Birdie sit up straight. She put her hand right on the heart of her Jesus T-shirt. What was the matter with her? How could she let her daddy go to war without even a real goodbye? Jesus would never do that. Being scared that someone would die was not an excuse. At Bible Camp, Reverend Colston had told them that Jesus gave his friends a long, beautiful goodbye message the night before he died.

She jumped out of bed, stuck her feet into her bunny slippers, and raced out of the house . . . just in time to see the old Subaru swing around the corner. She was too late.

When she turned, still bawling, to go back to the house, Gran met her holding out her jacket.

"Sweetie, here. Put your jacket on. It's freezing today."

Without a word, Birdie shrugged on her old Salvation Army Store jacket. She couldn't talk. She'd already said

8

too many wrong words before she even got out of bed this morning.

Birdie went back into the empty old house, went to her tiny room, pulled off her jacket, and got into bed. Once again, she pulled the pillow over her head. There was nothing else to do. She lay there trying not to think, but the view of the disappearing car kept rattling around in her head. Mom was driving him to Essex Junction, where the guard was gathering for the ceremony. Then the soldiers would get on the buses to the airport, from where they'd fly to some base and on to Iraq, where they'd all die.

She grabbed the pillow with both hands and smashed it down harder against her face. She would never see her daddy again. She didn't cry. She was too scared and mad to cry, but the pillow kept her from screaming out loud.

Later—it might have been minutes or hours, who cared?—Gran came in. Well, it was her house, thought Birdie, so maybe she thought she had the right to come busting in, invading somebody's privacy. Birdie wanted to tell her to go away, but she just pinched her lips together under the pillow and didn't say anything, even when Gran sat down beside her on the narrow bed.

"Elizabeth?" Her grandmother never called her Birdie. That was Daddy's name for her. In the story she begged him to tell her over and over again, he would tell her how much he and Mom had longed for their very own baby, so the very first sight of his own little birdie was the happiest moment of his life—right up there with the day he married Mom. It didn't matter to Birdie that he'd called her that because she was skinny and didn't have any hair and was always squawking to be fed. She loved that Daddy called her Birdie. Elizabeth was the name her parents used when they were unhappy with her. Gran said it wasn't respectful to call a beautiful, almost grown-up girl Birdie.

"Elizabeth?" Gran said again. "I made some cocoa. Would you like some?" From under the pillow, Birdie shook her head.

Gran patted her shoulder. When Birdie didn't respond, Gran sat there quietly for a minute before clearing her throat. "I'd like to make this room nicer for you while you're here—make you feel like it's really yours.

10

Would that help? I know it's small, but you could help me choose a new quilt or nicer curtains—something to make it look more like yours and not like the overflow space it used to be."

Exactly. How were you supposed to make a closet practically under the staircase friendly? Even Harry Potter couldn't do that.

"Well, I'll be in the kitchen when you feel like getting up." She gave Birdie another pat and stood up. "I think your mother will need cheering up this evening. I can't do that without your help."

She was gone at last. Birdie yanked the pillow off her head and rolled over on her back. The ceiling had stains on it from a leak that had probably happened before Birdie was born. You'd think in ten years a person could scrape together enough money to fix a ceiling. But it was always money. That's why they were all in this mess. In fact, Daddy had joined the guard in the first place just to bring in a little money.

Then came September 11, 2001. Birdie shivered and pulled the covers close to her chin, squeezing her eyes to shut out the sight of the flaming towers she'd seen

11

on TV. And after that came not one but two wars, and neither of them was over yet. Daddy had already gone to war twice, and now he was going again.

Even if two different presidents said both wars were nearly over, people were still going there and still getting killed. Lots of guys can survive one, maybe two deployments, but number three and BOOM! Of course, it had been that awful Warren Matson in Brattleboro who had whispered it just loud enough for Birdie to overhear in the lunchroom. Oh, if she could only unhear it.

Her grandmother was back at the door. "You haven't eaten all day," she said. "Let me fix you something. What do you want?"

What did she want? It was what she didn't want. First of all, she had never wanted a little brother. But mostly, mostly she didn't want her daddy to go to Iraq and die. She hadn't wanted terrorists to hit the twin towers, and all these years later, there were still terrorists everywhere.

Everybody said so.

She didn't want to go to bed every night wondering if she'd wake up in the morning. She didn't want to die.

And she would. Everybody did. People pretended that you wouldn't. Or they'd say, *only when you're really old and don't want to live anymore*. But that was a lie.

Why did grown-ups lie all the time?

Reverend Colston at Bible Camp said it was against the commandments of God to lie.

Gran was still waiting for an answer. "I'm okay," Birdie lied, and turned her face to the wall.

Well, God should know lying was different for kids. Sometimes they just had to lie.

She stopped herself. Suppose God was listening. Well, of course God was listening, stupid. God heard everything. She didn't mean she was so sick of the world that she wanted to die. No! She just wanted everything different.

Why couldn't God roll history backward as well as forward? Why couldn't He go back to September 10, 2001, and fix things so the next day was an ordinary sunny day in the fall and not the start of two wars and horribleness? If she was God, she'd sure run things differently.

Like press reset and let a new story take the place of the terrible one.

13

God wasn't going to do anything of the sort. Okay, so He wouldn't start over, like with Noah and the flood, but couldn't He just let someone in her family win the lottery or something so they'd have enough money and Mom didn't have to go to work while Daddy was overseas, so they wouldn't have to move to Gran's because rent on the apartment would be too high, and she wouldn't have to start in a brand-new school where she didn't have any friends?

At the thought of that—being alone and friendless, when God knew perfectly well that she was shy and had a hard time making friends (*remember that first summer at Bible Camp?*)—the rock inside her that had kept the tears dammed up broke loose. She began to cry like a baby, so loudly that she was sure her grandmother could hear her through the walls. She pulled the covers as well as the pillow over her head and cried into the black cave they made.

When the flood finally subsided, she wiped her nose on the pillowcase. Of course. That was it. That was what she had to do. Birdie sat straight up on the bed, then hesitated. Maybe with something this important,

14

she'd better kneel and show God she meant business. Reverend Colston always said it was good to kneel down when you prayed. It showed you were humble before God.

Birdie got down beside her bed. The covers tickled her nose, but she'd make the bed up after.

Now she put her hands together like that praying hands picture they hang in churches.

Okay, God. No. *Dear Heavenly Father.* That was better. *Dear Heavenly Father, I'll stop acting like a jerk, if you'll start acting like God and take care of us for a change.* No. *Erase that last part. I'll get up right up now and start acting normal if you'll . . . I mean, I will love you and Jesus and be a witness in the world if—if you will just keep my Daddy safe. Okay? Deal?*

Promise?

Love, Birdie. I mean, Amen.

Slowly she opened her eyes and stood up. Light was pouring through the one small window onto the floor. Light. "I am the light of the world." Jesus said that. It was like Noah's rainbow. A promise. God was telling her it was a bargain.

She sat down on the side of the bed. Her **I ❤ JESUS** T-shirt and pajama bottoms felt clammy, as though she'd been sweating as well as crying there under the covers. She grabbed her bathrobe and ran upstairs to the full bath. There was only a toilet and basin across from the closet room.

Under the hot shower she washed everything, her hair included. When she finished, she went back down to her room and laid out clean clothes. Although her **I ❤ JESUS** shirt wasn't exactly clean and was still a bit sweaty, she put it on anyhow. Her sweatshirt would cover it up so Gran wouldn't see it wasn't clean.

There, God, how's that? I'm doing my part. I'm clean and dressed. Oh, yeah, I mean, yes. Thank you for the sign. There. That should make God know she was really trying.

When Birdie appeared at the kitchen door, her grandmother was sitting at the kitchen table reading a book and drinking something from a cup—not a mug, a delicate china cup with a saucer under it. Gran was weird like that. She didn't have much money either, but she liked things like cups with saucers and the good silverware she'd inherited from her own mother.

"You're up!"

"Yeah."

"Feeling better?"

"Uh-huh." Mom would have corrected her. She liked for Birdie to say yes or no, not grunt an answer—especially when she spoke to grown-ups, most especially when she spoke to Gran, who used to teach high school English and liked proper speech. But Gran chuckled and said she was retired and wasn't about to start grading her granddaughter's grammar.

Well, Birdie wasn't going to mope and cry anymore. She had made a bargain with God there on her knees in the closet room. If she'd be good, step up to the dadgum plate like Daddy said, God would be good, too. Wasn't that what He had promised?

"I think I'll just have a bowl of cereal, if that's okay."

"Of course." Gran stuck a marker in her book and started to get up.

"I'll get it," Birdie said. "You're busy."

Birdie took down the box of generic cornflakes

17

Mom had brought from home and got the milk carton out of the refrigerator. They were out of bananas. She'd eaten the last one yesterday, and no one had felt like going to the store when they had such little time left with Daddy.

It's hard to do ordinary things when you are tiptoeing around God, trying to be almost perfect. You can't even complain about generic cereal. Birdie put extra sugar in the bowl to make up for the lack of fruit and ate most of the flakes, her elbow on the table and her head propped up on her hand. As she ate, she stared at her grandmother's bent head, her hair almost totally gray now and cut nearly as short as Daddy's. She never wore makeup or fancy clothes. Maybe when your husband has been dead for years and years, you don't make a special effort to fix yourself up.

She wasn't beautiful like Mom. Daddy said the first time he saw Mom, he thought she was the most beautiful person in the world. No, Gran wasn't beautiful. Not that she was ugly. She had a really nice smile, and sometimes Birdie thought she was actually pretty. And she wasn't all that old, was she? Sixty something? Seventy?

When Birdie had finished all she could swallow, she took the still-half-full bowl to the sink and rinsed out the soggy flakes. "Um, Gran?" Gran looked up. "I think I'll go for a walk." She couldn't think of anything else to do, and she didn't want to go back to bed. Not after her bargain.

"It's awfully icy out there."

"I'll be careful."

She had hardly walked a block when she realized that walking in this weather was crazy. It was well below freezing, and even with her hood up and her warmest mittens, the January wind bit into her face and hands. But she didn't turn back. And there, just ahead, she saw another sign.

Birdie gasped. It was a tree encased in ice. And even though the morning sun added no warmth to the day, it lit up the giant branches. They gleamed and sparkled. The thought came to her that the tree was singing, singing a hymn to the sun. She stood there looking at the great old fir, silvered and dancing, light sparkling from every branch. She caught herself listening for its song.

19

As cold as she was, and as anxious as she was, it was another message from God. She was sure of it.

Her grandmother heard the front door close and called out to her. "Ready for that hot chocolate now, Elizabeth?"

"Yes," Birdie said. "Thank you."

2

Alicia Marie Suggs

If Birdie had turned right at the corner instead of left, everything would have been different. Why had God let her do it? They had been getting along so well. He could have given her a little nudge when she got to the corner, but He hadn't. As it was, the first person she met that Saturday afternoon was Alice Suggs—or Alicia Marie Suggs, as she preferred to be known.

Birdie knew now that Daddy was really on the way to Iraq. Even with the bargain, though, it was too terrible to bear. She was trying not to cry. But when you're homesick and scared, it's hard not to. By the time she'd turned the corner and gone halfway down the next block, tears were freezing on her face. She rooted in her jacket pocket for a tissue and ended up wiping her eyes and nose, too, on the back of her mitten.

"What's the matter?"

Birdie jumped. The girl was sitting on the steps of a once-brown house, now badly in need of paint. "I said, what's the matter? Somebody die?"

"No!"

"You don't need to be so touchy. I saw you crying and I wanted to help. I'm often told I have a gift for helping people in trouble."

Birdie stared at the girl. She was wearing a neon-pink jacket trimmed with grayish fake fur. Despite the cold, her knees were sticking out from under a flowered cotton skirt, and she was wearing badly scuffed high-heeled blue boots that came halfway up her legs. After a few moments filled with nothing but Birdie's open-mouthed stare, the girl tossed the hood off her head and came down the short walk to where Birdie stood.

The girl's hair was what Birdie'd heard someone call dishwater blond, and it hung lifelessly down the sides of her narrow face. Her eyes were sort of blue, maybe more of a mixture that you'd think of as hazel. They were a little too close together and gave her the look of an irritated chicken.

"I said, what's eating you?"

"Uh . . . nothing," said Birdie.

The girl put her arm through Birdie's and smiled, revealing a mouthful of small, sharp teeth. If she could have, Birdie would have drawn back and gotten out of the girl's grasp, but she didn't know how to extricate herself in any way that wouldn't seem rude.

"I know who you are now," said the girl. "You're the one that's come to stay at Old Lady Cunningham's, right?"

"She's my grandmother," Birdie said stiffly.

"Oh. Right."

"It's just temporary—while my dad's overseas."

"No kidding! What a coincidence. My dad's overseas, too. What's your dad's rank?"

"I don't know. Corporal, maybe." Birdie had a vague memory of a promotion, but she wasn't sure to what.

"Oh. An enlisted man."

"He's in the Vermont guards."

"My dad—" The girl stopped a moment and examined her nails. She wasn't wearing gloves, and Birdie saw that the bright purple polish was chipped and peeling. "My dad," the girl continued, "is a full colonel—in—in the regular air force. You ought to see his medals. When I was little, I used to put them on—for dress-up, you know." She gave a little laugh as if dismissing her play as a child.

How old was this girl? Although she was a head taller than Birdie, she didn't have breasts yet, so she couldn't be much older than Birdie.

"You haven't started school here, have you?"

"No. No. Not yet. We just got here and my dad was leaving and it was the end of the semester and my—"

"What grade?"

"Huh? Oh. Uh. Fifth."

"What a coincidence! I'm in fifth, too." She gave Birdie an appraising look. "I figured you for younger. But, jeez, that's good. Maybe we'll be in the same class."

Birdie fervently hoped not, but she gave a weak

smile. *Screebies.* It would be just her luck. She wriggled her arm but failed to loosen the girl's grasp. "I gotta go," she said.

"Not yet." The girl squeezed even tighter. "You haven't even told me your name."

"Elizabeth," Birdie muttered.

"Do you prefer Bets or Lizzie?"

Yipes. Would this strange girl try to name her as well? "Most people call me Birdie."

"Birdie? That's cute," the girl said. "A little too old-fashioned and babyish for my taste, but then . . . I'm Alicia Marie Suggs, by the way. Of course, that's not my stage name." She laughed, a high prissy little laugh. "Only one of those country western stars would go by a name like Suggs."

"Stage name?"

"I'll tell you more about it when you aren't in such a gosh-awful hurry. Are you Cunningham, too?"

"Yeah." Birdie tugged again, but though Alicia Marie had the face of a chicken, she had the grip of a hawk. "Excuse me, but . . ."

"You don't have to be shy with me. We're going to be best friends, I can tell. People often say I have a special gift for friendship."

Birdie didn't ask what people, though she was surely tempted to. "I really got to go."

Alicia set her free with a final little pat. "Best friends, little Birdie!" She gave a wink. "I'm sure of it."

Birdie tried not to run, since the sidewalk plow had missed a lot of the icy spots, but somehow she had to get away from the strange girl—the girl who was so sure that they were going to be best friends. Birdie had friends in Brattleboro, but she'd never had anyone she thought of as her best friend.

She and Heather and Jamie and Melanie had kind of hung around together since kindergarten. She liked them, but none of them had cried when she told her she would be gone for at least a year. None of them had begged her to keep in touch. It would be hard to anyhow. She didn't have a computer, much less a cell phone, and the only letters she'd ever written were the thank-you notes Mom made her write to Gran for Christmas and birthday presents. Even if Birdie wrote one of them a letter, she might not answer, and how awful would that feel? No. They'd be busy with their own lives. They might even forget all about her. It happened. She was sure of that. She snuffled. She was not going to cry again.

And she didn't. Because things were different now, weren't they? She stepped carefully around a little patch of ice. Yes, everything was different. She and God had an agreement, a bargain—what did Reverend Colston call it?—a covenant. Yes, that was what God called bargains.

3

First Day of School

On Monday morning Birdie got up, put on her I ❤ JESUS T-shirt, her best jeans, and the new green sweater Gran gave her for Christmas, and came to breakfast.

"You're up." Her mother put down her coffee cup and smiled.

"I thought I'd start school," she said.

"I have to go to my orientation at the store this morning."

"I know. I thought Gran could take me. It might help if they know I'm her granddaughter."

Gran laughed. "Or maybe not. Most of my old students thought I was a pretty mean teacher."

"You always secretly like the ones who make you work hard," Mom said.

Her grandmother laughed again. "That's a nice thought, Susan. Let's hold on to that, shall we, Elizabeth?" Then she got up from the table and took one of those variety packages of little boxes of cereal from a cabinet. "Take your pick, love." She put the box on the table and went to the stove to heat milk for hot chocolate.

Birdie tore off the plastic wrap. Her hand hovered over the assortment. How could she choose from among the dozen little boxes? Mom had a funny kind of smile fixed on her face. She never bought variety packs. They were more expensive than the big boxes. She even bought generic cornflakes and wheat puffs. Never anything sugared or frosted.

It was as though Gran with her back to them could read their minds as well as see what was happening. "Don't worry. It's just a first-day-of-school treat. I won't make it a habit. When that batch is gone, it's back to oatmeal."

Gran loaded Billy into the stroller, and they walked through the cold and icy street to the school. It was old and had lots of steps up to the door. Gran had to pick up Billy and carry him up the long flight and into the office.

Mom had been right. The secretary at the elementary school nearly fell over herself when she saw Gran, and she gushed over darling Billy and even smiled at Birdie.

"Mr. Taylor is on the phone right now. Can't I get you something while you wait? Coffee? Tea? Juice?"

"Just a chair, please, Crystal," Gran said. "This boy is heavier than he looks."

The secretary rushed to get a chair from behind the counter and pushed it close for Gran to sit in.

"I don't know why this call is taking so long," Crystal said more than once while they waited. Finally, Birdie heard the principal say a formal sort of goodbye and hang up the phone.

"Nancy Cunningham!" He jumped to his feet when Crystal ushered them into his office. "It's always such a joy to see you! And with not one but two lovely grandchildren!"

Why did grown-ups, even school principals, lie? People always thought Billy was cute when he wasn't bawling, which, thank goodness, he wasn't at the moment, but no one except Gran thought she was "lovely."

"Sit down, sit down. I am so glad to see you."

"Even if . . . ?"

"Yes, despite the grade on my senior paper." He chuckled. "Forgiven but not forgotten."

Mr. Taylor then spent time fiddling at his computer to determine which section of fifth grade Birdie should go into. "All three of our fifth-grade educators are new to the area, so they wouldn't have known you at the high school."

"That's probably just as well," said Gran.

"No," he protested. "Their loss."

Gran gave Birdie a wry smile and said to her, rather than to the principal, "I gave a lot of less than flattering comments on papers. No one in town seems to have forgotten."

"Merv Goldberg," he said finally. "He's your kind of teacher, Nancy. I think Elizabeth will fit in well there." He stood up again. "Crystal will have some forms for you to fill out. Do come back soon. It's always so good to see you."

Gran said goodbye to the principal and stood up, shifting Billy to her other arm. When they were in the outer office, she said, "Birdie, would you sit down and hold him while I sign you up? I don't think I can manage both Billy and a pen at the same time."

Birdie sat down and, reluctantly, took the heavy baby from Gran. *Don't cry! Please.*

Please. Billy always cried when she was asked to hold him. This time, though, he looked up at Birdie wide-eyed, as though he was too surprised to cry.

Gran filled out what felt like endless forms. When Crystal asked about the records from Brattleboro, Gran dug around in her huge shoulder bag and retrieved Birdie's health certificate and report cards for placement in what Crystal was calling her new "permanent records."

Why would you call them permanent if they changed when you moved? That was the trouble with *permanent*. Nothing in this world was permanent—not friends, not jobs, not schools, not homes . . .

She tried to stop feeling sorry for herself, after all, but leaving Gran and Billy behind on the first floor and

32

following the secretary up the wide staircase to the third floor, she couldn't help it. What a baby she was! Daddy was off to war. All she had to face was a new school.

Fear not! That was always God's message in the Bible.

The staircase was stained and worn, and the stairwell needed a new coat of paint. The old paint was as gray as the stuff that pooches out of the neck of the vacuum cleaner bag. Why couldn't they paint the walls a bright yellow like a sunny day? Wouldn't everyone like school better if the walls weren't so goldurn ugly?

They finally stopped climbing. The secretary pulled open the heavy fire door at the top of the stairs and motioned for Birdie to go through. The hall was dimmer than the staircase as there were no windows. She waited and followed the secretary down almost to the last door.

"This is Mr. Goldberg's room," she said. "I called ahead. He's expecting you." The secretary smiled.

"Good luck." She turned to go.

So—she was supposed to take the last few steps completely alone, it seemed. Birdie pulled the door open and the light and warmth from the classroom engulfed her.

Okay, God. Here goes. She took a deep breath and walked in.

It was a large room with windows all across one side. The February sun was filling the room with light. There were no desks in straight rows, but round tables. The class was not as large as the one at home—twenty, more or less. She would count later. Mostly boys, though, drat it. Out of the corner of her eye, she caught Alicia Suggs grinning like a commercial for false teeth and waving from a table in the back. Birdie pretended not to see.

The teacher was a man! Well, of course. Crystal had said *Mr.* Goldberg.

Pay attention, dummy.

"Why don't you sit here, Elizabeth?" he said, pulling out a chair from a table near the window. Mr. Goldberg looked to be about Daddy's age. He had a nice smile and a lovely voice. It was like music, soft and warm without any phony gush. After Birdie sat down, Mr. Goldberg put his hand gently on her shoulder. "This is Elizabeth Cunningham, class. She won't remember everybody's name right away, so please introduce yourselves to her and make sure she feels at home with us."

34

There were four other people at the table. Three boys and one other girl. The girl, who was next to her, leaned toward her. "I'm Christine, but everyone calls me Christie," she said. "And that's Devon, Mark, and Wayne the Weird, but you can ignore them. I do."

Birdie smiled weakly.

"Do you have a nickname?"

"Birdie." She spoke in a whisper.

"Birdie?" Christie asked.

"You know, Chris, like in tweet, tweet," the one Christie had called Devon said in a raspy whisper. The other boys snickered. Birdie was blushing; she could feel it.

"Is there a problem, gentlemen?" Mr. Goldberg was back in front of his own desk.

The boys ducked their heads and grinned behind their books.

Ignore them. Christie mouthed the words.

Birdie was going to like Christie. She was really nice and pretty, really pretty. She had dark curly hair and brown eyes and didn't seem at all stuck-up. Maybe she'd become a friend.

But it all fell apart at lunchtime. Christie had brought her lunch and went to sit at a table with other girls from the class. As Birdie stood still, looking to see where the line to buy lunch began, she was grabbed from behind. "Over here, Birdie. I'm buying, too. We can eat together." And Birdie was trapped. She couldn't say to Alicia that she'd promised Christie to eat with her. She hadn't. And Christie hadn't really invited her to join her table when she'd found out Birdie was buying her lunch. So Birdie let Alicia drag her over to the line and stood there not really listening as Alicia prattled on about something. She couldn't help but notice that Christie and the other girls looked over from time to time to where she and Alicia were sitting, but no one came over to say hi or to introduce themselves.

"You haven't listened to a word I said!"

"What?"

"See? You're doing it again."

"Sorry. I guess I . . ."

"Just don't do it again, hear?"

Do what again? How could Birdie not do it again when she had no idea what "it" was?

She tried to listen to what Alicia was saying, but all the time she could feel the stares from Christie's table.

After lunch, Alicia showed her where to take her tray back, and then she linked her arm through Birdie's and walked her back up to the classroom. She didn't let go even at the door.

Birdie saw Christie look up and then quickly down. Birdie slid into her seat. "I see you and Alice Suggs are friends," Christie said.

She wanted to say something to Christie about not being actual friends with Alicia Suggs, in fact, hardly knowing her at all, but she didn't know how. "Not really. I just . . ."

"Well, I guess you get to choose," Christie said. "It's a free country."

But I didn't get to choose. I wanted you to be my friend, not her. But she couldn't say that. She couldn't say anything at all because Alicia had come over to the table.

"It's great you can come over to my house after school. I can catch you up on all the stuff you're behind in."

Had she told Alicia that she would come to her house after school? She couldn't remember saying anything

37

of the sort. She started to protest, but the teacher was speaking.

"Alice, would you take your seat, please?"

"Alicia Marie," Alicia mumbled, but she headed back for her own table.

When the bell for the bus rang, everyone from Birdie's table got up and left. Indeed, most of the class left. Alicia wriggled her fingers at Birdie from across the room. As soon as the second bell rang, she came right to Birdie's table.

"C'mon. Let's break outta here."

She followed Birdie to her cubby and waited while Birdie fumbled to get the books she had been given into her backpack.

"You gonna carry all that home?"

"I thought I'd better . . ."

"You're even more of a teacher's pet type than I thought." She sniffed. "Oh, well, suit yourself. But hurry. I need to get going."

"You—you don't have to wait for me."

"Remember? You promised to come to my house after school."

"I did?"

"Have you got Alzheimer's or something?"

"What?"

"Oh, come on. I'm just kidding. You've got to learn how to take a joke if you're going to hang around me. I'm known for my great sense of humor."

"I really can't go home with you. My grandmother expects me to come right home after school."

"We'll call her. Believe me, she'll be thrilled to know you made a friend already. She's probably scared you won't be able to make any friends here—you being so shy and all." She yanked Birdie's backpack up over Birdie's right shoulder and grabbed her arm. "Let's go."

Birdie pulled the other strap over her left shoulder. The books were heavy. Maybe she shouldn't have brought them all home. She'd probably get curvature of the spine or something carrying a backpack this heavy. Alicia didn't even have a backpack, or if she did, she certainly wasn't carrying it today.

Birdie didn't want to go to Alicia's house. She really didn't, but Alicia was pulling her along the sidewalk, chattering away. She hardly breathed, so there was no

39

pause, no opening for Birdie to say anything. When they got within a half block of the brown house, Birdie made herself interrupt the endless stream of chatter. "Is anybody home?" she almost yelled.

Alicia looked at her as though Birdie had lost her mind. "*I'm* home," she said.

"No. I mean your mother, some grown-up. My mother doesn't let me visit when there's no grown-up in charge."

Alicia whirled on her, almost nose to nose. "Oh, for crying out loud! What kind of a baby are you, anyhow?"

Birdie shrank back.

"Besides," Alicia said, "who's going to tell her?" Alicia started walking again. "C'mon."

Birdie had to skip to keep up. All the *but*s that were in her mouth got stuck behind her teeth. She didn't want to do "it" again, did she? Besides, she would be eleven in May, plenty old enough to be trusted in a house without a grown-up. Heather, in Brattleboro, was already babysitting her little brother, and she was barely eleven.

Alicia had a string around her neck, which she pulled out, revealing a house key. She fitted it into the lock of the doorknob and pushed the door open wide. "Go on in," she said. She sounded impatient, so Birdie went in.

The house was dark and smelled moldy. "Do you always keep the shades down?" she asked shyly.

But Alicia ignored the question, throwing her coat on the hall floor. "Aren't you going to take off your jacket?"

"I got to call my grandmother. She'll worry."

"Relax, will you? I got it covered." Alicia started down the hall. "And shut the front door, will you? Want to let all the heat out?"

"I'm sorry," Birdie said, although there wasn't a lot of heat in the house to let out. She shut the door carefully and slid off her backpack. The floor didn't seem very clean, and she hated to throw her jacket down, so she put it on top of her pack.

"What's the phone number?" Alicia was yelling from a room down the hall. Birdie followed the sound into a kitchen where Alicia was standing with a phone in her hand. "The number?"

Birdie whispered her grandmother's number. Alicia

punched it in, then pulled up her sweatshirt and covered the phone. Birdie could hear the four rings and then Gran's hello on the other end. Alicia moved several feet away and turned her back.

"Mrs. Cunningham? How are you? This is Melinda Suggs. Suggs. Alicia Marie's mother? Yes. Birdie's right here. We live just around the block in the old Simpson house. I'm sure . . . yes, that's it. Alicia Marie would love for Birdie to spend some time with her this afternoon. Yes, I'll make sure she's home before dark . . . She's a lovely child. I'm sure she and my Alicia Marie are going to be great chums. No. Thank *you*, dear. Goodbye."

Alicia turned around with a wide grin on her face. "She swallowed it whole." She brought the phone back and put it in the cradle.

"Chums?" Birdie didn't like the idea that Gran could be so easily fooled. "Chums? Nobody says chums."

"Nobody *we* know, but they always say it in the old books. Like Nancy Drew. They all had chums. I'm sure that's what made her think I was really old." She began to laugh and stopped abruptly. "You know our name really isn't Suggs, don't you?"

42

"No, I thought you said . . ."

"See, actually, we're French, but our name is so diffi-
cult for Americans to pronounce that my grandfather—
he had royal blood, you know—he thought he ought to
take an American-sounding name. Besides"—here she
bent over toward Birdie and whispered—"besides, with
a new name, it was less likely that they could find out
where we were . . ."

"They?" Birdie found she was whispering as well.

"Shhh." Alicia went to the door and peeked into the
dark hallway as though there might be someone in this
very house, lurking in the shadows. Then she straight-
ened, smiled cheerily, and said, "I'm starved, aren't you?"

Birdie nodded, although to tell the truth, her stomach had felt queasy ever since she'd entered the house.

Alicia cracked open the refrigerator door, but even
so, Birdie could see that it was crammed full of take-out
cartons and pizza boxes. "You want Chinese?"

"No, not really." She did like Chinese, but not
Chinese left over from who knew when.

"Me neither." Alicia shut the refrigerator door and
went to a cabinet to pull out a box.

"Hey, Pop-Tarts. I'm really in the mood for Pop-Tarts, aren't you?"

Birdie nodded. Actually, she hated Pop-Tarts. They were too sweet, but she was afraid saying so might be doing "it" again.

"Chocolate. My favorite. Don't you just adore chocolate?"

"Sure." She did love chocolate, just not in Pop-Tarts. Something seemed to happen to her favorite flavor when it dropped into a toaster.

"Delicious, isn't it?" Alicia said, chewing her Pop-Tart with her mouth wide open.

Birdie nodded. It seemed like less of a lie if she just nodded. Even if God meant for her to be here, He surely didn't mean for her to lie.

"Well, eat it, then."

"It's hot." A lame excuse, but the best she could come up with.

It didn't matter. Alicia was already stuffing the last of her Pop-Tart into her mouth. "Let's call someone else," she said, spitting out a bit of her mouthful as she spoke.

"Who?"

"Oh, just anybody. Here, hand me that phone."

Birdie put down the tart and got the phone for Alicia.

Alicia seemed to study it for a moment before she punched in seven numbers.

"Who're you calling?"

"Shhh. It's ringing. Pooh, it's going to the machine. Oh, well. Plan B." She waited for the message to play out, and when the talk signal rang, she again put the bottom of her sweatshirt over the phone and said in a husky voice, "You know who this is, and if you don't call back, you know what will happen. But if you call this number, you'll be very sorry. Use the other number. You know what I mean." She gave the off button a triumphant punch. "There! That should give them the willies."

"Who?"

"How should I know?"

"But you said . . ."

"Honestly, you are so innocent, it's almost sweet. Don't you know, everyone has some secret they don't want anyone else, especially their family, to know about? You leave a message like that, and you'll have the whole house in an uproar. Everybody will be suspicious of everybody else. At the same time, they'll drive themselves crazy trying to remember what number they're supposed to call."

"But you didn't leave any number at all."

"Of course not. Did you think I'd want those maniacs calling here? And just in case they have Caller ID—which my mom has blocked out for this phone—but if it accidentally slips through, they'd be too scared to call it."

Birdie's head was spinning. She was so confused, she picked up the Pop-Tart and took a large bite.

"Aren't you finished yet?"

"I really got to go home."

"You haven't even seen my room yet."

"Another time. Right now . . ."

"Tomorrow." It wasn't a question.

"Sure." Anything to get out of there. "Sure, tomorrow." She stuffed the rest of the tart into her mouth and headed for the front door.

Alicia followed her, hands on hips, watching as

Birdie put on her jacket and slung her backpack onto one shoulder and opened the door.

"Tomorrow. You promised, now."

Birdie nodded, her mouth still full of Pop-Tart. She pulled the door after her and raced down the steps, looking back to see Alicia's nose pressed against a pane of glass beside the door.

4
Be Ye Kind

It had been a hard first two weeks of school, between her worries about Daddy and her discomfort at school with Alicia clinging to her like a burr and the boys teasing her. Mom was exhausted at work, and Gran was going nuts trying to make Billy happy. She'd vacuumed the life out of the living room rug so she and Billy could get down on it and play together.

Billy wasn't all that interested in playing.

And even though Saturday had come at last, it wasn't going to be any better. The Dollar Store was making Mom work for the entire weekend. "Well, I am the newest hire," Mom said, as though she was apologizing for the giant chain.

"That's a shame," Gran said. "I was hoping the three of us could do something together. Gloria Shelton is begging for a chance to sit with Billy."

"I guess you two will have to have fun without me."

"There's not a decent movie showing at either theater," Gran said. "At least nothing suitable for . . ."

"It's okay," Birdie broke in. "I got this invitation from Alicia. She wants me to come over."

Gran smiled. "See, Susan? You don't need to worry. Elizabeth has already made a friend."

Mom whipped around. "Where?"

Why was she so nervous all of a sudden? "At school," Birdie lied. "She's in my class. She asked me to eat lunch with her, and—and then we found out we lived just around the corner from each other."

"I think it's all right, Susan. Her mother called last Monday when Elizabeth stopped by there after school."

"Do you know this family?" Mom demanded.

"Well, no, not yet. They're new. They're in Elaine Simpson's old house—the brown one on Elm Street." Gran didn't seem worried. If there was something fishy about the Suggses, she'd know it. Neighborhood gossip was sure to have reached her ears, even if she wasn't the sort of person who passed it along.

It wasn't that Birdie wanted to go back to Alicia's house, exactly. It was just that she didn't want her mother getting all protective and treating her like a baby. She was plenty old enough to pick her own friends. Besides, Gran wasn't worried.

"When were you planning to go over?" her mother asked.

"I dunno." Birdie shrugged. "Sometime later this morning."

"Be back in time to eat lunch with Gran, okay?"

"Okay. Okay. You don't need to worry, okay?"

"I'm sorry. It's not you, sweetie. I'm just . . ."

"Let's just sit down and have a nice breakfast. You have a hard day ahead of you, Susan. We have to fuel you up." Gran smiled and headed over to the coffee maker.

Mom smiled, too, a little weakly, but she smiled and patted Birdie's arm. "Be patient with me, sweetie. I'll need a lot of help from you to get through this year."

"Sure, Mom. It's okay." *Who's supposed to be the grown-up here?* Birdie thought, and then immediately

50

felt ashamed. She needed to put on her Jesus T-shirt. It had been a little sweaty to sleep in. She went back to her room, took off her pajamas, and dressed. The T-shirt was now safely under her old sweatshirt.

Alicia called before they'd even finished breakfast. "Yeah, I'm coming," Birdie muttered into the phone. "Don't worry. I'll be there after I finish eating, okay?"

She waited until Mom left for work. The car sputtered and coughed and finally started.

Birdie noticed for the first time there was rust under the back passenger-side door.

"So," said Gran after the car disappeared. "What's your plan for today? Staring out the window?"

Birdie turned. She didn't think Gran meant to sound mean, but it felt a little like it. Birdie really didn't have a plan. Alicia had a plan. It bothered her that Alicia hadn't even asked if Birdie wanted to come over on Saturday— just said she was. She wasn't at all sure she wanted to spend more time with Alicia—or Alice, as everyone else seemed to call her. "You will call me by my real name: Alicia Marie," Alicia had said. And there was the problem of nobody liking Alicia or Alice or whatever her name was. Christie had been downright icy when she saw that Birdie was with Alicia.

"Be ye kind, one to another." That was one of the verses they had used all the time last summer at Bible Camp. She'd gone to Bible Camp three summers in a row. It was cheaper than a babysitter, Daddy had said, and since both of her folks worked, they needed to fill up Birdie's summer with time-consuming activities.

She'd gone to day camp at the Y, which was cheap, and the library summer program, which was free but only lasted until noon. Bible Camp was a sleepaway camp run by one of the local churches. The pastor, Reverend Colston, was the director of the camp. Everyone in town knew Reverend Colston. He'd been at the Community Christian Church for twenty-eight years. He was known for his kind heart.

"Sure, he's a bit on the conservative side," Dad had said, "but he's a really fine person."

"She's never stayed away overnight!" Her mother had protested it. "And she's barely eight." *As though Daddy didn't know her birthday was May the fifth.*

52

"She'll be fine," Daddy had said. "Plenty of fresh air and time with nature. It'll be good for her. She'll learn how to be independent."

The first summer she'd nearly died of homesickness, but she didn't tell them. She wanted so much for Daddy to be proud of her. He was so brave. He even emptied mousetraps. One time the mouse was still wiggling, but he didn't let that stop him. He just grabbed the wriggly mouse by the tail, took it down the outside staircase, and let it go in the backyard. And now, *now*, he was going to war and he wasn't a bit scared. Birdie and Mom had to be scared for him. Somebody had to be.

So, trying to be brave for Daddy, she went back to Bible Camp the next summer. It wasn't nearly so bad when she was nine and knew some of the kids from the previous year. And everyone had to be kind to everyone. The Bible said so.

Counselor Ron, who was new last summer, seemed to think kindness was overrated. He made sure his camp group understood about judgment and that the Bible also said you had to believe right or you would go to hell. He showed it on a flannel board. He stuck on flannel people with wrong beliefs and then put the flannel flames of hell right on top of them. It was all just pieces of cloth, but still it was scary, and it made Birdie wonder if she believed right or not. Just in case, she had bought an **I ❤ JESUS** T-shirt from the camp store so Counselor Ron wouldn't wonder. It took all her snack money for the week, but she figured the insurance was worth it. She hadn't realized until last year's camp that from then on, she would have to worry about not only whether she was going to heaven or not but where everyone she loved was going to end up.

And despite her bargain with God, this was one of her great fears, even though she kept squashing it down. Not only was her Daddy in danger of dying in the war; if he died he might go straight to hell. That's what Counselor Ron had said to their group at camp. That you had to believe right or you were in danger of hell's fire. She'd been too scared to ask Daddy if he believed in Jesus the right way. Suppose he said no or *let me think about that* or something squirrelly like that? What could she do? Her bargain with God might go straight out the window. Well, she *thought* God had agreed to it. You couldn't be sure about God. He was tricky.

"If you don't want to go to this girl's house, you don't have to, you know."

Birdie shook herself like a dog, shaking off her thoughts. "What?"

The *br-iiing* of the phone interrupted the conversation. She knew at once who was calling. "I'll get it," she said, glad not to have to think any more about what Gran had said or about what was the right way to believe.

"Hello."

"Where are you? You said you were coming over this morning. I can't believe you forgot."

You said I was coming over this morning, Birdie corrected in her head, but not out loud. "I didn't forget. I been tied up. I'll be over in a few minutes, okay?"

Alicia was waiting on the porch in her pink jacket. "Well, finally," she said, and turned and opened the door.

The house seemed even creepier in the cold light of the winter morning. "We're having Pop-Tarts," Alicia announced. "Chocolate. Your favorite."

Birdie wasn't sure she could choke another Pop-Tart

down. Her throat felt like sandpaper. "I just ate," she said, but Alicia ignored her and plopped two tarts into the kitchen toaster.

"It's good chocolate are your favorite, because that's all we have today. Mom ate the last raspberry before she left this morning."

She didn't want to ask where Alicia's mother worked, because she was sure it wasn't at the Dollar Store.

"She had to see our agent," said Alicia, answering a question that hadn't been asked.

"Are you selling your house?" The only agents Birdie knew about were real estate agents.

Alicia laughed. "No, no, dummy. Our *personal* agent. The guy that represents our act. He's negotiating a gig in Las Vegas for us."

"Oh." Birdie didn't get it. She didn't even know what a gig was, but she didn't want to be called dummy again.

"You probably haven't heard of our act. You'd have to be really sophisticated to know about it. Do you read *Entertainment Weekly*?"

Birdie shook her head.

Alicia sighed. "It sounds like bragging, maybe, but you won't know about it if you don't read the trade papers. We were recently featured in *EW*. That's what we call *Entertainment Weekly*. The Seran Sisters. My mom is so young and beautiful that no one believes she has a teenage daughter."

Seran sounded more like a plastic wrap, and Birdie was sure Alicia wasn't yet a teenager, but it was clear Birdie knew nothing about show business, so she let the questions drop and tried to get a hunk of dry Pop-Tart down her unwilling throat.

"Well, hurry up with that tart, or just bring it along. We need to go to my room and plan my costume for Las Vegas."

Birdie looked around desperately for someplace to pitch the rest of the tart, but there wasn't a trash can in sight, and, besides, Alicia might catch her doing it.

It was hard to concentrate on planning a costume, but it was obvious Alicia didn't need ideas, only an audience. "You see, it's got to be sophisticated, but, at the same time, I want it to really have, you know, pizzazz."

57

So outfits were considered and rapidly discarded as either not sophisticated enough or lacking the proper pizzazz.

Birdie wanted to ask what pizzazz was but didn't.

The monologue was interrupted by a loud slamming of the downstairs door. "Alice!" a woman's voice yelled. "Are you up there?"

Both girls froze.

"Is that your mom?" Though why would Alicia's mother be calling her Alice and not by her real name?

"You gotta go," Alicia said, jumping to her feet.

"Huh?"

"You gotta go home. Uh . . . um . . . Mom and I will have to talk about the gig—you know, the one the agent set up."

"Oh. Okay." Birdie stood up as well. "I'll just get my jacket."

There was stomping of feet in the downstairs hall and more yelling.

"Don't make me come up there, Alice May!" Obviously, the person thought "Alice May" was "making her come up there," because the next noise was the sound of someone stomping up the stairs.

"Stay here!" Alicia commanded, then ran out and slammed the door almost in Birdie's face. She wasn't sure what to do. Go? Stay? The yelling decided it. She went back and perched on the edge of Alicia's unmade bed.

"Okay, Mom, okay. You don't have to yell." Alicia said it so loudly that it came straight through the closed door. There was another noisy exchange. Birdie couldn't make out the words. There were strange noises, even more than just the yelling. Surely no one would hear her if she left now. She crept to the bedroom door and opened it a crack. She strained to hear her own name through the din, but there was too much yelling and banging to make out any actual words. Then she heard the yelling go down the short upstairs hall. A nearby door slammed shut.

Birdie tiptoed into the hall and, stopping to listen on every step, made it down the stairs. Silently, she retrieved her jacket from the hall table and headed for the door with her jacket over her arm.

The door was heavy, and the jacket slid almost to the floor as she grabbed the knob, but she couldn't take the time to stick her arms through the sleeves. She

59

needed to get out before anyone caught her escaping. It took both hands to pull the door open and close it behind her with only a gentle click. Then she was free.

Birdie raced down the steps and ran down and around the block before she stopped to put on her jacket.

5

Finding Anne

Birdie was still breathing hard when she walked into Gran's house. She'd hoped to get to her room before she was spotted, but just as she got past the living room archway, Gran called out to her. "Hi! Have fun?"

At first she didn't see Gran when she looked into the room. She wasn't sitting in her reading chair. No, Gran was on the floor on her hands and knees opposite Billy, who was up on all fours. Laughing. Actually laughing, for a change.

"Um. Her mom had something for her to do, so I left early."

"I see," said Gran, although it was pretty clear she didn't. "I was wondering why you came back so soon."

Gran stumbled to her feet and then leaned down and picked up Billy, whose lips had already begun to tremble. "No problem there, I hope."

"No," Birdie said, edging her way down the hall toward her own room. "Not really. Just—" *Just what?* "Just a mother-and-kid thing. You know."

Gran might have said something else, but Birdie didn't wait for it. She went into her closet of a room and shut the door. There was no place to sit—just the bed. She lay down and stared up at the stained ceiling. She was a prisoner in that tiny room, but it felt safer than any place outside. She wished she'd thought to bring something inside to read. Despite all the books in the living room bookcase, Birdie didn't have a book or even a magazine in her room, and, of course, no radio, much less a cell phone with games on it like Heather and Melanie had. No way Birdie's folks could afford a phone. "Well, anyhow," Daddy had said, "I don't really want you playing games all night long like some kids I've heard of."

She tried praying. She reminded God about their bargain, how she'd be good if He kept Daddy safe and

62

brought him home. Should she pray for Alicia? She might have gotten Alicia in trouble by going over this morning. It felt like it. The way Alicia didn't want her mom to see that Birdie was there.

The room was too chilly for just her **I ♥ JESUS** T-shirt, but Birdie needed to feel closer to it. She peeled off her long-sleeved shirt and sweatshirt, and although she had goose bumps, it made her feel better. And God was sure to approve. But she was soon really shivering, so she pulled the covers back and got into bed. There was nothing else to do. No books, because, as Mom often reminded her, "The library is free." And, of course, no games, no dumb phone for that matter (but who would she call?), no game she could play on the TV. Daddy had even suggested it, but Mom had said no. She didn't want Birdie monopolizing Gran's only TV, and it was so old, any new game Daddy had bought probably wouldn't work on it anyway.

She was asleep before she knew it.

Gran woke her up for lunch. She hadn't had anything but part of that awful Pop-Tart since breakfast, so she must be hungry, mustn't she? Gran was trying to put baby food into Billy's mouth, but he was spewing most of it back out. It was disgusting.

Birdie ate a mostly silent meal of grilled cheese and tomato soup. Did Gran ever get to eat? Well, what could Birdie do about that? Nothing. "May I be excused?" she asked politely.

"Are you feeling all right?"

"Just sleepy." She wasn't really sleepy, but she sure didn't want to sit in the kitchen and watch Billy not eat.

"In the upstairs hall there are a lot of old children's books," Gran said. "Some of your dad's, some from when I was young, and even some I picked up over the years to see what my students were reading." She grinned. "Quite a variety. Why don't you go up and see if there's a book you might like?"

Well, it was something to fill the time. Birdie climbed the stairs. The hall was dark, and she couldn't remember where the light switch was hidden. These old houses. Why was everything, even just turning on a light, so hard? She could see the bookshelf. It wasn't that dark, but it was hard to make out the titles of the books. After her eyes adjusted, she could begin to tell that Gran had sort of arranged the books in sections. There was a science section. No. Those books were fake. They would all probably try to say that evolution was true, and Counselor Ron had really warned them about that. She went to what seemed to be the fiction section. She knew perfectly well that witches and fairies weren't real, but Counselor Ron had also warned their group that all those creatures were devil-inspired and books about them not fit for Christian children to read.

Charlotte's Web. Something warm went through her stomach. She remembered that book. Daddy had read it to her years ago. She remembered snuggling into his big, warm body. She could feel the vibrations of his voice in her own little body. She put it back on the shelf. She knew it would make her cry to read it again. Even Daddy had cried, she remembered suddenly. It was the only time she had ever seen him cry. It scared her. But he just patted her with the back of his hand that still held the page open. "It's all right," he said gently. "I can't help crying when Charlotte dies."

No, not a book about dying. Besides, it wasn't true.

Spiders can't write and pigs can't talk. It was also a fantasy, and Counselor Ron had warned them about the evils of all kinds of fantasy. She'd tried to ignore that when Daddy was reading *Harry Potter* last fall. Reverend Colston had reminded all the campers that the fifth commandment said plainly, "Honor thy father and thy mother." Listening to your daddy read you a story was surely honoring your father.

She dragged her fingers across the book spines like they were piano keys.

Surely there was something—something true but not scary or sad. She sat down cross-legged to reach the bottom shelf. Almost at the end of the shelf, her finger stopped. It was a book written by—well it looked like a real person; there was a photo of a real girl on the cover. *The Diary of a Young Girl.*

Birdie had once started keeping a diary herself. In fact, she still had it somewhere. It was a present from Santa. (Another grown-up lie.) She'd begun writing in it after Christmas last year. But her life was so boring—she kept saying the same thing every day. The only change was what she'd eaten for supper. She gave up writing in the middle of January. Besides, she hadn't been much of a writer when she was younger. This year she was much better.

She'd dig the diary out of the box of stuffed animals and things she'd brought here from Brattleboro. Maybe if she read how some other girl had written a diary, she could make her own diary more interesting . . . She wouldn't lie, of course, but really, with Alicia in her life, would she need to lie? If her diary only said what Alicia had done or said that day, it would be interesting— puzzling, maybe, but certainly interesting. And she'd remember, and could tell Daddy about it

Birdie started to get up off the floor, but then another title caught her eye. It was about God. *Are You There God? It's Me, Margaret.* That was funny. She didn't think Daddy would have had a book about God when he was her age, especially one where a girl was talking to God. Maybe it was one Gran had. Mom and Daddy had gone to church off and on and taken her to Sunday school. But once Billy was born, they hardly went. People at Bible Camp would have had plenty to say about that, especially Counselor Ron, who thought Congregationalists weren't really Christians. Mom and Daddy didn't say much about God even when they knew Daddy was going off to war. You'd think that would make you more religious—at least, you would want to pray, wouldn't you? She pulled that book off the shelf as well. Then put it back. If Margaret was full of doubt, maybe it wasn't a good time to have to worry about someone worrying about God.

She went back and got *Charlotte's Web*. No matter what Counselor Ron thought, it was a really good book.

Which to read first? She took both downstairs. She could see Gran in the kitchen, Billy on one arm and a bottle in the other. "Oh, you found something," Gran said.

Guts! She wished Gran wouldn't keep track of her every move. *Guts* was Ramona Quimby's favorite cuss word, so it couldn't be too bad.

"Yeah. I mean, yes. I got a couple." She kept walking toward her room. She knew Gran would want to know the titles, but, really, she didn't have to know everything, now, did she?

Now. The diary or *Charlotte's Web*? Neither one

was all that long, and she had the rest of Saturday and Sunday, and oh, cripes (she apologized to God—she really was going to stop cussing), but it did stink that Monday was Presidents' Day and no school because of that, either. Okay, a few pages of one—say the diary one—to remind her how to write a diary so she could get that started right away. *I mean, if this girl's diary was good enough to be actually published as a paperback book, it has to be a good role model for how a diary should be written, right?* Maybe she should have chosen the God book after all. If she read it, it might give her some good advice on how to save Alicia. Jesus said not to judge other people, but even so, Birdie was pretty sure that Alicia didn't know Jesus yet.

Maybe that was why God had brought her here. He was calling her to bring Alicia to Jesus. She hadn't thought of that. Why hadn't she remembered what Reverend Colston said, that God always had a plan? He even had a plan for her, Birdie's, life. But the more she tried to figure that out—I mean, surely God didn't cause the whole Iraq war to start so Birdie could save Alicia.

That would mean God made Saddam Hussein and

69

George W. Bush be heads of countries so that . . . No, it didn't make sense, but still—here she was. If she'd turned the other direction on her walk, everything would have been different. *Show me thy path.* That was one of the prayers they'd learned at camp. God has a path for you, and you ask God to show it to you because if you get on the wrong path, Counselor Ron said, you're headed down to you-know-where. She didn't even like to say the word because, after all, it was practically a cuss word.

Well, thankfully, she wasn't going to see that girl today. There'd be a whole, long, terrible year to explain the Plan of Salvation to Alicia Marie Suggs. Surely, today, she could read whatever she wanted to.

6
The Secret Diary

Birdie plumped her pillow and leaned it against the headboard, stretched out on top of the covers, and opened the worn paperback. She skipped the introduction. That was always some grown-up telling you what to think. She didn't want anyone telling her that (except God, of course) and jumped to the first sentence of the actual diary: "I hope I will be able to confide everything to you, as I have never been able to confide in anyone, and I hope you will be a great source of comfort and support."

Birdie almost cried out with joy. Anne Frank knew exactly how it was. That obviously was the reason to keep a diary. It had to be secret. It had to be your secret friend. She kept reading. Anne was going to name her diary Kitty and pretend that she was writing her friend Kitty letters, so if anyone got nosy and didn't respect her privacy—and grown-ups hardly ever did—they would just think she was writing letters to a friend, not keeping a totally secret diary.

Birdie sighed. She closed the book. Before she went any further, she had to find her own diary. She could tear out the boring pages and start all over again. She would, of course, give it a name. But not Kitty. That was Anne's private name.

"Gran, do you know where that box of my stuff from Brattleboro got to? There's something I need in it."

Gran was sitting in the living room reading. She must have put Billy down for a nap. Was he supposed to have a bottle and a nap now? Well, it wasn't Birdie's problem. She wasn't in charge of the baby and was certainly not the boss of Gran.

"I think all those boxes are in the basement." Gran put her book down on the side table and started to get up. "Do you want help looking?"

"No!" Then less sharply, "No, thanks. I can do it."
Screebies! Birdie was sounding just like Mom. Mom
never wanted help doing something she thought was *her*
job. Daddy said they nearly got into a fight at college the
very first time he ever saw her because he tried to help
her pick up broken dishes off the dining hall floor.

It was dark in the basement. Where was the freaking
light? She almost stumbled right down the stairs to the
cement floor. And where would that leave her? Probably
crippled for life, that's where. *Sheesh!*

Then she remembered. The blamed switch was outside the basement door. She turned around and groped
her way back up the dark staircase. These big old houses!
Nothing made sense in them. The apartment had been
small, but at least you could find the light switches. Billy
had to sleep in her parents' room, as there had only been
two bedrooms—well, in this huge house there were
still only two *real* bedrooms. Billy was still sleeping in
Mom's room, wasn't he? While Birdie existed in a closet
like Harry Potter.

Daddy had only been halfway through reading the

first Harry Potter to her when he got called up. They'd had to return it to the library. She'd probably never know what happened.

"The switch is on the right side of the door," Gran called.

"I got it!" All she needed was Gran coming to fuss over her. She started down the stairs again, but she left the door wide open this time. The bulb was dim, but at least she could see the steps.

The boxes from home were neatly stacked against the wall at her left. Not far from the stack hung a bare bulb, screwed into its own socket with a short chain coming down. She stretched up on her tiptoes, but she couldn't reach the chain. Well, she wasn't about to ask for help looking for her diary. That would blow everything. Gran would say something like how nice it was that she was keeping a diary and then tell Mom, and they'd discuss it either at the table or behind her back or . . . She had to have some privacy. And, well, criminy! Weren't diaries supposed to be secret? What was the point if there wasn't anything secret about them? Why else had hers come with a latch and a little gold-colored key?

Oh, no. Where had she put the key?

Well, one problem at a time. Which box was hers? And would she be able to pry it out from the neatly stacked piles? The military had made Daddy start liking order. If only Mom had been in charge of stacking. There would have been no stacking, probably at all. Still, Dad would have labeled the boxes and kept things separate. She knew Mom. Mom would have just pitched things in any old way and forgotten what was in what box. "We creative types have trouble with organization."

She'd heard her mom use those exact words a million times. Always when something went disappearing in the apartment. Dad had just laughed. "That's probably why I married you," he said. "So I'd always have a little creative chaos in my life." Of course, if Birdie had been more like Daddy and less like Mom, she would know exactly where she had put her diary key.

It was good to be creative. Maybe not so great to be creatively messy, but creative was good. She wanted to be creative. Mom used to be a really good painter. She hadn't painted much lately. Paints and paper were expensive, and since Billy was born, there was now a crib, a changing table, a jump seat, a diaper pail—all that junk taking up the space where there used to be room for an easel and stool. The little chest that used to hold art supplies now was stuffed with onesies and baby junk with packages of disposable diapers on top and falling off onto the floor. Babies took up much more room than they ought to. The smaller the kid, the more room they took.

And now Birdie was stuck in a closet. *Stop complaining and concentrate.*

There had to be labels, and if Daddy was going to stack the boxes, he would have written the label where somebody looking for a particular box could see it. Yes, there was definitely writing on the sides of the boxes. She squinted, trying to read the neat printing on the boxes at her eye level. She'd have to get a stool or something to look higher and get down on her knees to read the ones at the bottom. He sure hadn't been thinking about her wanting her box anytime soon the way he had stacked them. And it wasn't as if the boxes were all the same size either. He'd apparently just gotten empty boxes from behind Walmart or Shaw's, wherever they were free. She hoped they didn't have cockroaches or something in them. She shivered. It was cold and a bit spooky in the basement.

She was still squinting and scanning when she heard footsteps over her head and then, sure enough, Gran calling from the top of the stairs. "Need a hand down there? Those boxes are stacked higher than your head."

She was opening her mouth to say no, but it was too late. Gran was already coming down.

"Oh, my goodness, you can't even reach the light." Gran walked over and pulled the short chain on the bulb near the boxes. "That's better. Now. What are we looking for?"

She wanted to say *nothing* or *I can do it* or even *none of your business*, but what she said instead was: "The box from my room at home."

"Let's see." Gran started at the top, tiptoeing to read the high labels. "He seems to have marked everything pretty carefully."

Birdie was reading the lower boxes, now that she could actually make out the writing. "Here it is!" She felt as though she had won the game somehow. She, not

Gran, locating the right box. It was on the very bottom, however, with lots of stuff on top.

"Oh, boy," Gran said, coming to stoop down to where Birdie was pointing. "Louis is a smart man, but he didn't think about the fact that an old woman and a ten-year-old might be trying to pull out a box from the bottom of the mountain. I guess we'd better not risk just yanking it out. The whole arrangement might come tumbling down on us."

She began to tug at the box on top. "Your father used to build block towers and try to pull one block out of the bottom without the whole shebang coming down. He ought to know better." She stood up on her tiptoes. "Let's hope this high one isn't too heavy." She stuck her fingers around either side of the box and began to pull gently. "It says china. Keep your fingers crossed."

Birdie held her breath. They didn't own any really good china, but still . . . Gran had the box halfway out and tilted. "Okay," she said. "Get out of the way, Elizabeth. I don't want to drop this set of breakables on your head, which is also fragile."

Birdie jumped back, still hardly daring to breathe.

Gran eased the CHINA box out and, holding the bottom firmly in both hands, got it safely to the floor. "Whew. One down, two to go. The next box was labeled UTENSILS, and Gran was able to easily dislodge it and put it on the floor. KITCHEN MISC was larger and heavier but not a problem, as the distance to the floor was measured simply by the medium-size box marked BIRDIE'S ROOM.

"Finally," Gran said, and stepped daintily around the boxes littering the floor to let Birdie pull her own box out.

"Thanks," she said softly. She knew she couldn't have done it without Gran, but she couldn't make herself say that. Her box wasn't very heavy. It was mostly stuffed animals, which was why, probably, Dad had thought it safe to put on the bottom. But shouldn't he have known she needed her things? She shoved away the disloyal thought. "I'll take my box up, and then I'll come back and . . ."

"No, no," said Gran. "I'll just push these out of the way so the meter man won't trip over them when he comes. You go ahead. It'll make your room more like home to have some more of your own things in it."

As if anything . . . But she didn't finish the thought. Gran had helped her find her box.

Once in her room, she kicked the door shut and put the box down by the bed. It almost filled the narrow space between her bed and the small bureau that stood against the opposite wall. She knelt down beside it and began ripping off the tape. Why had Daddy put so much on, anyway? She needed some of those tape slicers that they used at the grocery store.

The flaps were finally free and she could open the box. There at the very top was a large animal that might have been a bear or maybe some unknown stuffed animal species that had been a gift at her baby shower. Her earliest memory of the creature was that it had scared her, and she'd never really liked it. But you couldn't just put an animal in the trash can. When Mom suggested that she give it to the Salvation Army, Birdie had been sorely tempted, but she couldn't shake off the feeling that the poor, ugly thing would hate her for such a desertion. So here it still was, taking up most of the box even though it had been bent and squashed to fit in.

Like me, she thought glumly. *Bent and squashed to*

fit in. But once the beast—she'd never named it—was out, oh joy, Pooh the Bear gazed up at her as lovingly as ever. She had renamed her beloved bear after Daddy had read her *The House at Pooh Corner*. How could she have let anyone cram him into a dark box and hide him in a basement? Nestled into Pooh were Biff the Bunny and Little Lamb and several of a neighbor's hand-me-down Barbies that Birdie didn't play with—just dressed and undressed and dressed again. They had no real life. They never did anything. There was no Ken to provide romance or marriage, no house to live in. They were just plastic dummies like the ones in the store, only plastic dummies for old, rather shabby miniature clothes. But under these smaller toys, she could see a gleam. It must be the latch on her diary.

She pitched the dolls and stuffies on the floor. She was too old for them anyway, except for Pooh, who did have a life, a real life with books about it.

She lifted out the diary carefully, as though it was fragile. She looked into the empty box. No key. She ran her fingers into the corners to make sure.

Nothing. Without much hope, she pushed the little

brass button. A miracle. The latch gave way, and, there, inside the cover was a small, sealed envelope with her name on it in Daddy's neat printing. She tore it open. When she unfolded the note inside, the key fell out.

My little Birdie, the note read, not in his neat block printing but in cursive.

> *I confess. I thought you didn't like the diary I gave you for Christmas last year. Yes, I'm terrible, I peeked. But you do like it because you've taken the trouble to find it. I hope you'll write in it all you're doing while I'm away. It will help you count down the days, and when I'm back, help you remember everything I missed about your life while I was far away. I'll want you to catch me up on every single detail. Please forgive me for being so sneaky.*
>
> ♡ *Love, love, love,* ♡
> *Your Daddy*

He'd also drawn a lot of little hearts for love even though he'd always teased her when she used a heart instead of writing out the word. Like in **I ❤ JESUS**.

She read the note all over again. She loved his funny scratchy cursive that was almost half printing. So even though they didn't teach how to read real handwriting in school, she could read her daddy's words. She kissed the wobbly hearts he'd drawn. It was almost as though he was sitting right there on the floor beside her, teasing her with his smiling eyes.

"Thank you, Jesus," she whispered. "Please keep my daddy safe. Even if I'm not good, he is. You know he is."

She put the note back into the ripped envelope and the envelope into the back of the diary and locked the latch. She would ask Mom to find her a ribbon. Then she'd hang the key around her neck so nobody could steal it, and she wouldn't lose it. The diary wasn't going on the floor. She opened the small drawer in the stand beside her bed and put both the book and the key inside. She would return the box to the basement later. First, she laid the Barbies and most of the stuffies in the bottom of the box. She folded the legs of the beast onto its awful head and crammed it in on top. *Sorry, Beast, but you are just too ugly to stay in the same room with my . . . my*—she needed a name for her now-precious book.

And almost like magic, she had it! The perfect name: Betsy, because it was a secret name for Elizabeth, her real name, and Lou, for Daddy's Louis. *Dear Betsy Lou, this year we're going to be best friends.*

7
The Color Green

Birdie had stayed up late reading *Charlotte's Web*. She couldn't stop because all the words came out in Daddy's voice. Between finding his note and starting her diary—just like Anne did—she felt closer to Daddy than she had since . . . since when? Since the day he left for Iraq? Since they left Brattleboro? Since before Billy had been born and there had been just the three of them in that tiny upstairs apartment? She wasn't sure. She only knew how close she was feeling to him as she read about Charlotte and Wilbur. *"Some pig!"* She giggled out loud. *Some Daddy!* She had no idea what time she'd fallen asleep.

"Are you awake, sweetie?" Mom was at the door in the stupid uniform she had to wear.

Birdie jerked wide awake. The lamp beside her bed was still on. "Is something wrong?"

"No, it's nearly eight thirty and I have to get going." Mom came over and switched off the lamp. "Can you help Gran with Billy today? I know she usually goes to church, but someone has to take care of the baby while I'm gone."

Birdie never wanted to take care of the baby, but after all, she'd be eleven in less than three months.

Mom saw the hesitation. "I think you're both too young for solo babysitting. A couple of months, maybe. When we all feel more settled. In the meantime, you can be a big help." She gave a crooked smile, blew a kiss, and was gone.

While Birdie dressed, she could hear the sounds of Mom giving Gran last-minute instructions on the care and feeding of babies—like Gran hadn't raised Daddy and didn't know all about babies. Honestly. Sometimes her mother didn't have the sense she was born with. Mom was out the door before Birdie came into the kitchen.

"I see you're wearing your favorite shirt," Gran said,

waving a spoon in front of Billy's face, trying to make him take a bite.

Birdie blushed. "Yeah."

"Well, if you're worried, I love Jesus, too."

"I wasn't worried," Birdie lied.

"I'm not much for wearing slogans across my chest." Gran laughed. "For that matter, I can't remember the last time I wore a T-shirt or even a sweatshirt. I'm not sure I own either one anymore. In my day, the authorities didn't encourage teachers to dress like students. I think the situation is more informal now." It was a dumb conversation, but Birdie didn't know how to improve it.

"I think the eggs are still hot," Gran said. "Can you serve yourself? I seem to be tied up here with your brother, who is a reluctant eater." Billy responded by spraying the spoonful Gran had gotten into his mouth right back at Gran. "Oh, come on, Billy Boy," she said, wiping her face with a cloth diaper hung over the side of the high chair.

Birdie made herself a piece of toast and sat down at the other end of the table to eat. Babies were such a mess. She was fairly sure, now that Billy had come and disrupted their lives, that she would never have one of her own. She hadn't even liked playing with dolls all that much. She should probably have a career and become famous. She wasn't sure yet what she wanted to be famous at, but certainly not famous as someone's mother. You had to be somebody like Abraham Lincoln's mother for that to count.

She remembered then that Daddy had once said that when he was a kid, he had wanted to be a famous writer. "Is that why you type on the computer at night? Because you're a famous writer?" she asked. He had laughed. "Well, right now, I'm not even a *published* writer—unless you count my pieces in the Winslow College literary magazine." He had tousled her hair. "But I keep trying. I want to write really good stories that people will read, and someday"—he was looking off someplace near the ceiling—"someday I want to write the Great American Novel."

She didn't like hearing him sound sad. She wasn't even sure what the Great American Novel was, only that it was something that would make him really happy. "You'll do it," Birdie said. "You can do anything."

Daddy laughed. "You're my best cheerleader," he had said. Birdie knew what a cheerleader was. She'd seen them at the football games on TV. She liked thinking of herself in a swirly skirt, yelling at hundreds of people to cheer for her famous daddy.

When the phone rang, Birdie jumped. Why did she always think if the phone rang it would be bad news?

"Could you get that, Elizabeth?"

"Where are you?" the voice demanded. "We had a date."

Birdie glanced over at Gran, but she wasn't listening. "I'm sorry. I thought after yesterday . . ."

"Are you coming or not?"

"I . . . uh . . . I'm kinda busy today. I told my mom I'd help with the baby."

"What baby?"

"My baby brother."

"You didn't tell me about any baby brother."

"Well—well—"

"You gotta tell me these things. We're besties. I need to know all about you if I'm gonna help you."

Birdie hadn't thought she needed help—certainly not from Alicia.

"Why can't your grandma watch the kid?"

"I'm, I'm s'posed to help."

"Oh, c'mon. How much trouble can a baby be? Get your grandma on the line. I'll fix it."

She carried the phone over to Gran. "She wants to talk to you." Birdie was careful not to say who the "she" was. No telling who Alicia was going to pretend to be.

Gran mostly nodded. "No, of course, Mrs. Suggs. If the girls had planned . . ." More nods. So Alicia was her mother this morning. "All right. No, lunch isn't necessary, thank you. I'd like to have her home by one for . . ." Nod, nod, and—was Gran actually rolling her eyes? "Yes, yes, all right . . ." Billy started to yell right then, as if, all of a sudden, he was interested in the blinking green goo from the baby jar. "Yes, but you can hear that I really need to . . ."

Gran pointed the phone back in Birdie's direction, shaking her head. *Interesting woman,* she mouthed rather than said aloud.

"I fixed it. She didn't suspect a thing. Old people can be so dense," said Alicia.

Birdie wanted to protest, to say her gran was really smart, but somehow she didn't. Anyhow, if she went over to Alicia's, she was sure to have something to write in her diary besides a description of Billy's face smeared in green goo.

Alicia met her at the door. "Shh," she said. "My mom's still asleep. She had a late night. Well, we both did. Club in Burlington. We're only performing there to polish the act."

Did clubs let kids in the door? Much less perform? It didn't seem right . . .

"I pass for twenty-one," Alicia said. "We call it a sister act because Mom looks so young for someone in their forties. And most people think I'm over twenty-one."

Could Alicia read her mind? It was a worrisome thought.

"Quiet now." Alicia was whispering and walking in her sock feet. "Take off your boots and bring them along. Jacket, too," she commanded when Birdie started to slide hers off. Birdie obeyed. She seemed always to be obeying Alicia, even though the Bible only told you to obey God and your parents. But God obviously wanted her there in Alicia's house. Otherwise, He would have made her turn right instead of left the morning she'd first seen Alicia. Maybe God had sent her like a missionary to Alicia, who worked in night clubs and was probably lost.

Alicia closed the bedroom door behind them. "Now, take off your jacket. That's not a good color for you, by the way. You should tell your mom to get you a pink jacket. Green makes you look pasty."

Birdie had never particularly liked the jacket. Mom had gotten it at Salvation Army. She bought a lot of their clothes there. She thought the quality there was better than at Not New, and the prices were about the same. Although Birdie had wanted a new, not-used jacket, she had accepted it, but then, she hadn't realized it made her look "pasty." She thought of the big jars of kindergarten paste. Really?

She was surprised to realize that the room was warm, really warm.

Yesterday, Alicia's room had been cold. The whole house had felt cold. But now . . .

"Yeah, better, huh? I brought the space heater out of Mom's room. She won't miss it. She's sound asleep." There Alicia was, reading her mind again. It was spooky. "Where does your mom come off buying green for you?"

Birdie had forgotten that once she peeled off her jacket, she would reveal her pullover, which was also green. A different shade, but still unmistakably green. "It was a present. Gran gave it to me for Christmas." She was aware of how defensive she sounded, but she loved the sweater. And it was new, out of a regular store, and she didn't want Alicia saying it made her look like kindergarten paste and ruining it for her. She took it off quickly.

"Holy cow! Who the hell gave you that T-shirt?"

Birdie looked down at the shirt on her chest as though she'd never seen it before. At least it wasn't green. It had once been a gleaming white, which made the huge red heart really stand out, but in the dim light of Alicia's bedroom, it looked gray and apologetic.

"Hel-LOW! I asked you a question."

"I—I bought it myself."

"You *what*?"

"I bought it." Now she was really sounding defensive. "I got it at camp. All the kids had them."

Alicia rolled her eyes elaborately. Did she have some kind of junk on them? They looked huge. Yes, eyeliner and mascara. A bit smeared, too. "We've got a lot of work to do, girlie. You are in *big* trouble."

Alicia was the one in trouble. Wasn't she? Going to night clubs and wearing makeup when she was no more than eleven years old. Mom and Daddy would have a fit, and, according to Counselor Ron, they probably weren't even true Bible-believing Christians. Birdie shivered. She didn't want to think about that. Besides, Alicia was the one God wanted Birdie to save. Surely God Himself would save Mom and Daddy. He had to. They were so good.

"Put your sweater back on. I can stand you in green better than I can take that stupid saying on your chest."

Birdie put the sweater back on. It was better to be hot than to feel like she was letting Jesus down by not taking up for her belief in him.

"Now. Sit. Here." Alicia pushed her down.

The chair was hard, and a broken spoke poked Birdie's back, but she was afraid to complain. Besides, Christians needed to suffer for their faith. She had to show Alicia that she was strong and uncomplaining, didn't she?

"Shut your eyes. I'll tell you when to open them."

It seemed like hours. She tried praying, but her mind wandered as it often did when she tried to pray. She wasn't good at praying. Did that disappoint God? Make Him angry? Maybe she should have kept her mind on the constant babble coming straight into her face from Alicia, who never stopped talking—mostly about all the plans she and her mother were hatching for their show in Las Vegas next month. What was Alicia doing to Birdie's eyes? Her face? She caught a few phrases now and then—"romance theme," "all about love," "that's what our fans want."

It was obvious Alicia and her mother both needed saving. But Birdie couldn't worry about Mrs. Suggs. Dealing with Alicia alone was going to be more of a challenge than she'd realized.

"Okay! Wow!" The exclamations jarred Birdie to attention. Alicia was fumbling to put the handle of a mirror into Birdie's hand. "You can look now!"

Her eyelids felt stuck together, but she pulled them open to see a person in the mirror who looked like one of those strange old women who think dyeing their hair and wearing lots of makeup makes them look younger.

"Great, eh?"

"Are you saved, Alicia?"

"Wh—aat?"

"Are you saved?" She needn't have asked twice. The look on Alicia's face made it quite clear that Alicia had no idea what Birdie was talking about. *Thank you, God. I'll do my best.* She took a deep breath, only to have Alicia exclaim:

"What's got into you? *Jesus!*"

Alicia made the name of Jesus sound like a cuss word, but Birdie tried to hide her shock.

She was on a mission. She had to think fast. What had Reverend Colston said? How you should approach a nonbeliever? With gentleness. She took another deep breath . . .

"Come on, stop daydreaming!" Alicia's knuckles were rapping on her scalp. "Wake up! Tell me how you like your great makeover!"

"My what?"

"Your new look. I wish I had my cell so I could have taken before and after shots like in magazines. But it's in the shop today. I'm having it upgraded." She stepped back from the chair, hand on one hip, and cocked her head. "I don't care what you think, Birdie. I love it."

"Very nice—uh—job, Alicia." She shouldn't lie just when she was trying to talk about being saved to a lost soul. But she knew she had to talk fast or the devil would make Alicia keep interrupting and changing the subject.

So without hardly taking a breath, she recited the whole Plan of Salvation, just like Counselor Ron had drilled it into their group at camp. It was thrilling. She could almost hear Counselor Ron's voice taking over her own as she explained fast as machine gun fire how you keep from going to hell when you die if you believe what the Bible says—that Jesus died for your sins. She grabbed a quick breath. "You don't want to spend eternity in hell, do you, Alicia?"

Alicia was staring at Birdie with her mouth open so wide Birdie could see that she was missing a back tooth. "Hell? What the . . ."

Whatever Alicia was about to say was interrupted by a yell.

"Alice May! Get your butt over here!"

"You better go."

Birdie grabbed her boots and her jacket and started for the door. "Will you think about it, Alicia? About believing in Jesus, I mean?"

"Sure, sure. Now get outta here!"

From the room down the hall, the yelling started up again. Alicia practically shoved Birdie out the bedroom door and stayed on her heels, steering her along the far side of the hall so she was nowhere near the closed door and the yelling.

Birdie tiptoed down the stairs with Alicia practically pushing from behind. It was hard to get into her boots without sitting down and with Alicia breathing down her neck and the yelling coming down the stairs as loud as ever.

"Can't you ever hurry?"

Birdie could only nod and yank at her boots. When they were most of the way on, she hobbled to the door. Alicia already had it open and slammed it shut as soon as Birdie was over the sill.

Birdie stood on the porch and put on her jacket over her even greener sweater. Did they make her look pasty? Never mind. Caring about her own looks was false pride. She shook off the temptation of pride. She didn't even try to figure out what was happening on the other side of that door. No matter. Her heart was beating fast. Birdie had actually preached the Word. Alicia had heard the message of salvation and promised to think about it. God was sure to be pleased. Despite all the scary yelling and the push out the door, if the sidewalk hadn't been so icy, she would have skipped back to Gran's.

8
Betsy Lou

Dear Betsy Lou,

Finally, I have something interesting to tell you about.
I went to see my friend

Should she say "friend"? But what else?

Alicia Marie Suggs today. She doesn't think I look good
in green. She said it made me look pasty. I didn't mind
about the jacket because it came from Salvation Army,
but the sweater is new from a regular store. It's soft and
a really nice shade of green. Greens are different, as you
well know, and all of them couldn't make me look funny,
could they?

Another thing. Alicia saw my I ♥ JESUS shirt and just about had a cow. But I think it's because she doesn't know Jesus as her personal savior, not because she's like Gran, who doesn't believe in wearing slogans on her bosom. Although "I love Jesus" is not a slogan. It is a declaration of personal belief, and we need to stand up for Jesus whenever we can. But then I realized why God sent Daddy to Iraq and made us move here. God wants me to save Alicia. I mean, she's all about makeup and Las Vegas and pretending to be grown-up enough to get into a bar. With makeup and a padded bra, she might pass, but it would be a lie.

Speaking of makeup, I forgot I had it on until I walked into the house and Gran saw me with all that stuff on my face. I thought for sure it would freak her out, but all she did was smile and say something like she could tell us girls had had a lot of fun with Alicia's mom's makeup. OF COURSE I didn't tell her that it was Alicia's makeup and not her mother's.

Speaking of her mother, there is something funny (and I don't mean ha-ha funny) about Mrs. Suggs. Whenever I'm over there, she is either gone or asleep or yelling. Maybe that's how famous people act. I've never met a famous person in my life before Alicia and I'm not sure how famous she is. But then she's always telling me what to think and do and wear. I guess that's how it is to be famous. You get to tell everyone else what to do. It might be nice to be famous. I can't tell anyone what to do. It might be better to be famous after I grow up. I don't know what I'd be famous for, but it wouldn't matter much, just so long as I was famous and people loved me and did what I told them to. I wouldn't want adoring fans. Nobody should be adored except God and Jesus. But it would be nice to have lots of people loving me and thinking I was great.

God wouldn't mind that, would He? Maybe I could be like a famous woman evangelist that brought thousands of lost souls to Jesus. Wouldn't that be a good way to be famous? Great evangelists have their own television shows that people all over the world can see. Then I'd even be more famous than Alicia, but I'd let her come on my program and give her witness. She wouldn't have on lots of makeup and be wearing slinky clothes. She'd just be dressed nice.

102

Maybe I'd ask her to sing a praise song, and then she could tell how when she and I were both little girls I had brought her to Jesus. She had been on the road ~~to hell~~ to a bad life when God like a miracle brought me to Gran's house and turned me to the left instead of the right that morning so we met. Yes, brothers and sisters, she would say, the Bible says a little child will lead them, and believe me this little child led me to salvation. Praise the Lord.

I would be wearing a long green robe, which, it turns out, is the perfect color for my complexion and looks good on TV too, and we would hug right there before the cameras and the TV audience of millions and all the people in the huge church where I was the full-time preacher. Everybody would be crying tears of joy like God does over one sinner's repentance.

I gotta go. Gran is calling me to lunch and speaking of crying, Billy is at it again. He cries too much, don't you think? Is he missing Daddy or is he too little to understand? Talk again soon.

Love,

~~Birdie~~ Elizabeth

9

Blessings and Curses

Considering everything, things hadn't been going too badly for a whole week. Since the makeover Sunday, Alicia hadn't made her come to the brown house any afternoon. And Alicia hadn't called on either Saturday *or* Sunday demanding that Birdie come over. At school, Birdie was so busy partnering with Christie on their social studies project that she didn't have time to pay any attention to their rowdy tablemates, and class time had become almost peaceful. Maybe Wayne and Devon were tired of teasing her so much. Or maybe they had run out of ideas. They didn't seem to have a lot of imagination.

Even though she and Christie never ate lunch together—Alicia made sure of that—during class time, Christie had been super nice as they worked on their project. It was about the European Union. She and Christie had made little flags of all the member nations. Christie brought toothpicks from home, and they attached the flags and planted them in the right countries on the map of Europe they'd drawn and colored. Mr. Goldberg thought it showed a lot of initiative.

And now it was Monday morning of a brand-new week. Birdie hadn't had a chance to read more about Anne or even to reread *Charlotte's Web*. She had spent practically all her waking hours studying up on the European Union, which had, if you asked Birdie, too many dadgum countries. But it had been worth it to bask in Mr. Goldberg's praise of her and Christie's project and be almost-friends with Christie. Never mind that Alicia was bummed.

Birdie woke up feeling good and looking forward to the day for a change. Mom and Gran were already up and in the kitchen. She could hear their voices. She decided to wear her green sweater. She had to wear her green jacket. She only had the one. But she decided then that Alicia wasn't right about everything. If she wasn't right even about the most important thing, God, then she might not be right about colors, either.

What was really going on with Alicia, anyway? Since the day she'd done Birdie's makeup and then rushed her out the door so her mom wouldn't know Birdie was there, Alicia hadn't invited Birdie to come to her house at all. Not that Birdie was disappointed at that. She didn't like Alicia's house. It felt all wrong. It was a relief not to make those strange visits. She looked at herself in her green sweater in the bathroom mirror and smiled.

When she came in for breakfast, her mother was at the kitchen table trying to get cereal into Billy. It was all over his face and bib, but at least it wasn't green. She suppressed a giggle. Green was definitely not Billy's color. He shouldn't wear so much of it.

"Oh, I'm so glad you're wearing that sweater," Mom said, looking up from the sticky spoon to greet her. "It's such a nice one."

"Do you like me in this color? Green, I mean?"

"Absolutely. Don't you agree, Nancy?"

106

"That's why I chose it. You look smashing in green, Elizabeth."

"Really? You don't think green makes me look . . . um, pasty?"

"Pasty?" Her mom's face screwed up like she was smelling something funny. "Wherever would you get that idea?"

Gran was smiling. She knew whose idea it was. "These girls." She shook her head. "Don't believe everything you hear, Elizabeth. It might just be jealousy talking."

Jealousy? Could Alicia be jealous of her, Birdie? She dismissed that crazy idea immediately. "I guess I better eat." She had hardly sat down when the phone rang.

"It's your friend," Gran said, bringing the phone over to Birdie.

"Where are you? You said you would be here at eight sharp so we could walk to school together."

Birdie was sure she hadn't said anything of the sort, but—Birdie sighed—that was Alicia for you. She looked at the big kitchen clock. "It's only quarter till," she said. "I'm still eating my breakfast."

"Well, get a move on. You know I don't like to wait."

Birdie handed the phone back to Gran. "I guess I'd better hurry."

"Your lunch is here on the counter," Gran said.

Birdie was eating as fast as she could, so she just nodded.

"Were you planning to buy lunch today?" Gran asked. "Sorry. I had that leftover meat loaf, and you seemed to—"

"No, no. That's good," Birdie said, although she was sure it would make Alicia mad that she wasn't buying. Alicia always bought.

"At last," Alicia said. "Honest. You got the worst memory of anybody I know. You said eight sharp and I said okay, and now, here it is almost eight fifteen, and the bell rings at eight thirty, in case you forgot that, too."

"That's just the first bell," Birdie said defensively. "We won't be tardy until the nine o'clock."

"That's when all the losers jam the doors. As you should know by now, the right people are there when the first bell rings. Up until you came, I have always gone in at the eight-thirty bell."

"Oh. Sorry."

"Just see it doesn't happen again. Now hurry. Honestly. You're the slowest person I've ever met."

And Birdie was wearing her green sweater. Alicia would think she was a double loser. Then, of course, Alicia got mad again at lunchtime because Birdie had brought her lunch.

"Doesn't your stupid grandma realize we're supposed to buy?" Alicia gave a gigantic sigh. It sounded like when you let all the air out of a blown-up balloon. "Well, the least you can do is save me a seat."

Birdie found an empty table close to the end of the cafeteria line. Before Alicia had even gotten close to the tray station, Christie and her gang came past on the way to their usual back table. They all seemed to be carrying identical brand-name lunch bags. Birdie smiled shyly at Christie, who smiled back. After all, since the triumph of their project, they were almost friends. And then, to Birdie's amazement, Christie stopped.

"You by yourself today? You could join us."

"Um." It was the very invitation she had longed for. Birdie had almost jumped to her feet before she remembered: Yield not to temptation. It would surely be a sin to put her own desires before God's plan, so without looking at Christie, she said, "Alicia's coming."

"Oh, yeah," said Michelle with a sneer. "Alice. Enjoy the company." And they all, including Christie, walked on to their table.

It seemed forever, sitting there, all alone, waiting. She should look like she was thinking about something fascinating. She stretched her mouth into a dreamy smile, or something she hoped anyone looking would take for a dreamy smile.

She closed her eyes. Maybe when she opened them, Alicia would have finished buying her lunch, and she wouldn't have to sit here all alone. She peeked. No, Alicia wasn't quite up to the tray station. But it wouldn't be much longer. She squeezed her eyes shut.

"Ow!" At the punch on her arm, her eyes popped open. The boys from class were standing close to the table, laughing.

"Who did that?" she snapped.

"Guess!" they were laughing their heads off now. Every head in the lunchroom turned their way.

"Leave me alone!"

"No worry, Tweetie," said Devon. "Just trying to keep you from falling asleep on your sandwich."

They were still laughing as they headed for their usual lunch table. She had felt so good when she woke up this morning, and now it was all ruined. She didn't close her eyes again. She didn't fake-smile. When she caught someone staring at her from another table, she glared right back. She hated this dumb school. Nobody liked her.

Blessed are you when men revile you and persecute you and utter all manner of evil against you falsely for my sake. Well, she was being persecuted for Jesus's sake, wasn't she? She wouldn't be in this dumb school and this dumb town if God hadn't wanted her to come here and save Alicia. *Rejoice and be exceeding glad, for great is your reward, for so persecuted they the prophets who were before you.* It was one of Reverend Colston's favorite verses. Birdie wasn't sure she wanted to be persecuted like the prophets or to wait to die to get her reward in heaven, but still, right now, it was a very comforting verse. Surely, God had brought it into her mind in her time of need, as Reverend Colston had said God would. She would try to rejoice and be exceeding glad like the Bible said. She really would.

"See what happens when you bring your own lunch? Those guys are a big bunch of losers." Alicia used the end of her tray to shove Birdie's lunch bag farther down the table and then swung her legs over the bench to sit down beside her. "Don't do it again."

Birdie knew Mom wouldn't let her buy lunch every day, and she would never apply for free lunch or subsidized lunch, Birdie was pretty sure of that. Just how did Alicia always have lunch money? If her dad was really a colonel or she and her mom made lots of money singing, they might. Well, it was not something she was going to ask about right now.

Alicia was saying something, but she was talking with her mouth full and didn't seem to notice that Birdie hadn't heard a word she was saying after the stuff about

112

buying lunch. Birdie'd missed the chance to explain about not being able to buy every day, maybe hardly any day.

The only good thing about the afternoon was the last half hour, when Mr. Goldberg always read aloud. Even though Counselor Ron said Christians should only read books about real people who had good morals, she couldn't help liking this one about a brave little mouse who loved an actual princess. She didn't want to be a mouse, but, oh, oh, she so wanted to be brave.

Birdie pretended to take a long time after school at her desk to make sure all the boys had left before she went out. Alicia was waiting outside the classroom door. The hall monitors didn't let people loiter in the building.

"Jeez. I thought you'd never come. I have things to do, you know, besides standing around all day for you."

Birdie was pretty sure *jeez* was a cuss word, but it didn't seem the right time to tell Alicia, so she just said, "Sorry."

"I planned to have you over today like I know you wanted, but I can't," Alicia announced as they walked along. "Mom and I have a lot to do to get ready for Las Vegas."

"It's okay." It had been such a relief not to go to Alicia's. And today—she just wasn't up to witnessing today. In fact, her well of witness was pretty near dried up. Birdie was exhausted. It was harder to stand up for Jesus and be persecuted for righteousness' sake than she had imagined. Maybe Reverend Colston and Counselor Ron were expecting more than they should from kids. Maybe the Bible was talking to grown-up Christians when it said you were supposed to be a witness all the time to the whole world.

She had a lot to figure out. She wasn't sure she was ready to have only one sort-of friend and everybody else either avoiding her or persecuting her. God had to know she was just a kid who hadn't been a real believer for all that long. Didn't he?

It was such a relief to open Gran's front door and throw her backpack on the floor and pitch her jacket on top of it. She'd pick them up later, but for now she just wanted to go to her room.

"Elizabeth? Is that you?"

Who else would it be, Gran? she wanted to ask, but when she glanced into the living room, Gran was not in her chair. She was sitting on the couch beside . . .

"Mom?" What was her mother doing home in the middle of the afternoon?

"Come in, sweetheart," her grandmother said.

She knew before they said anything. No one had to tell her. "Daddy's dead."

"No, Elizabeth, he's not dead, but he's been hurt. Pretty badly, it seems. They're flying him back to Walter Reed."

"Who's Walter Reed?"

"It's not a person," Gran said. "It's a big military hospital in Washington."

Birdie just stared at her blankly.

"Washington, DC," Gran said, as if that explained anything.

"You think he's going to die."

"No!" Gran said, then less sharply, "We don't know."

Mom turned at last toward Birdie. Her face was blotchy and her voice blurry with the tears she hadn't finished shedding. "We don't know anything."

"Well, what we do know is that your mother needs to get down there," Gran said.

"Me too. I need to go, too."

Neither of them answered her. She looked from Mom's face to Gran's. "I have to go. I gotta see him."

Mom sighed and shook her head. "They probably won't let you see him. Anyhow, we can't afford the air-fare even for me."

Gran opened her mouth as if to argue but thought better of it. It made Birdie sure that Gran had already said she'd pay, and Mom had said no. Stupid pride.

"Maybe when he's better—just not right now . . ." Mom's lips closed tightly over the words.

Birdie looked from her mother to her grandmother. They both wore the same stricken expressions on their faces.

"He is dying, isn't he? You're just lying to make me shut up."

"Oh, sweetie!"

"Elizabeth, no!"

Why did they think they could fool her? Grown-ups were always lying to kids. She was sick, sick, sick of it.

"I hate you," Birdie said. "I hate you both."

She was so shocked by her own words that she turned and ran back to her own room, slammed the door, and flung herself on the bed. She buried her face in her pillow to smother her sobs. God! It was all God's fault. He hadn't kept His side of the bargain. She had done her part. She had been so good it hurt. She had been a witness. She had suffered persecution for Jesus's sake. And God had not kept Daddy safe from harm. It was the least He could do, but, no, Daddy had hardly gotten to Iraq and God had let him be blown to bits. What kind of God was that?

Was God up there laughing at Birdie for being so stupid thinking she had a promise from Him? Or maybe there was just some big empty space and God was nowhere. *Oh, Daddy. Why did you go and leave me? You would have been safe at home with me and Mom and that baby boy you love so much. Don't you know how much I need you?*

Thinking this way made her cry even harder, hot, angry tears. She was mad, so mad, mad at God, at Mom, at Gran, even at Daddy, at everything in the whole stinking world.

117

10

Everything Will Never Be All Right

Mom knocked on her door. "Birdie?" Her voice was so quiet, Birdie could hardly hear it through the heavy wood. "May I come in?" Birdie pretended not to hear. Mom knocked again and called again softly, but Birdie didn't answer. Then Mom left, and Gran came and knocked and called. When she finally went away, Birdie jumped off the bed and turned the lock. She didn't want either of them just opening the door and barging in thinking—*ha!*—they could fix things.

Didn't they know that nothing, nothing could ever be fixed again? It's not like putting a bandage on a boo-boo. It's nothing that a kiss on the sore spot can make go away. Grown-ups always think somehow they can fix things. But they can't.

God can't even fix things. Or won't. Or maybe God is just a fairy tale, after all. *Are you there, God?* She made herself stop crying for a minute to listen.

Okay, God, this is a test. If you're really there, say something. "Speak now, for thy servant heareth"—that's what the boy Samuel had prayed, and in the Bible, God had spoken. Speak now or forever hold thy peace. Where had she heard that? It didn't matter. God was on notice to speak up or shut up.

Birdie was so quiet that she could hear through the door the murmur of voices from the living room. She heard Billy's waking-up cry. She heard Gran's voice shushing his cries. She heard Mom's step on the stairs and then over her head from the bedroom. Then footsteps going back and forth from the closet. Packing. She heard the belch of the furnace sending up more heat.

She heard squeaks and hums and traffic, but she didn't hear even a whisper from God. And she was listening! Really listening. Listening so hard her ears ached.

Birdie sat up on the edge of the bed and pulled off her green sweater. Next, she peeled off her **I ❤ JESUS** T-shirt and threw it on the floor. She looked at the dingy T-shirt for a moment. She had loved it once. Birdie smoothed out the crumpled sweater on the quilt before she crawled under it and closed her eyes.

Dear God, make Daddy . . . She stopped herself. There wasn't any God. She couldn't pray anymore. There was no one to pray to. She wanted to cry some more. Not for God. She was crying for herself. She was all alone. It was worse than being an orphan.

When her mom knocked to say she was leaving for the airport, Birdie got up and unlocked the door. She didn't know what to say to her mother's sad eyes. She couldn't tell her that God would take care of Daddy. She certainly couldn't tell her that there wasn't any God. There was nothing Birdie could say to comfort that sorrowing face. She just raised her own chin and let Mom kiss the tracks of tears on her cheeks.

"The taxi's here, so . . ." Mom leaned over and

pushed Birdie's hair back off her sweaty face. "I love you," she said.

Birdie nodded and snuffled. With the intake of breath came the familiar mother smell of lilac cologne. It almost started the tears again.

"Pray for Daddy, sweetie, and me, too. We'll both need it."

Birdie didn't have the heart to tell Mom that she knew, now, about God. So she just nodded again and tried to smile a lie. "Bye," she mumbled.

Her mother took Birdie's face in both her hands. "I love you so much, my precious girl," she said, her eyes filling up. She gave Birdie's face a gentle pat and then, turning quickly, went to the front door and out to the waiting taxi.

Birdie didn't follow her out or even go to the door to watch the taxi pull away. Instead, she shut her bedroom door and went back to bed.

When Gran called her to supper, she put her sweater on over her naked chest and crossed the hall to the kitchen.

Gran had set the table in there instead of the dining room, where they usually ate at night. So, it seemed, everything in her life was going to be different now.

Birdie picked up her fork and put bites of mac and cheese into her mouth and chewed and swallowed and took another bite, repeating the process like a robot even though it was like eating sawdust.

Gran had pulled her chair next to the high chair. She was feeding Billy—or aiming for his mouth and sometimes hitting it.

Birdie kept her eyes mostly on her plate, but sideways she could see that Gran was looking at her from time to time. Once in a while Gran would say something to Billy like "Open wide," but she didn't play airplane trying to land the way she sometimes did—the way Daddy nearly always did.

"I'm guessing the plane took off finally," Gran said. For a moment Birdie thought Gran was talking about Billy's spoon. How did Gran know what she was thinking? She looked up, puzzled.

"Your mother's plane to DC," Gran said. "There was a long weather delay."

"Oh."

"She promised to call when she lands safely."

Birdie nodded.

Gran aimed another spoonful at Billy's mouth. "You're a good little pray-er," she said. "Now's a good time."

All of a sudden everybody was wanting her to pray, it seemed.

After Gran waited a bit for the response Birdie didn't give, she said, "We're all needing a lot of prayer right now."

That meant Gran didn't know about God, either. That there wasn't one.

The next morning when Birdie went into the kitchen for breakfast, Gran was sitting in a chair with Billy in her lap, feeding him from a bottle. Mom thought he was big enough to drink from a cup at mealtime, but Birdie didn't want to remind Gran about Mom's rules. Not this morning, anyway. Gran's hair was all whichway and her eyes were bruised-looking and droopy.

Gran looked up as if to explain the bottle. "He cried

half the night. I think he's missing his mommy." She sighed. "So am I." She looked back down at Billy. "I hope he didn't keep you awake."

"No. It was okay." Birdie had slept. Maybe it should have kept her awake—everything that had happened and knowing God either didn't care or wasn't there at all. It didn't matter which, did it?

"I'm sorry," Gran said. "Can you get yourself something? The cereal is in the . . ." She pointed her nose up at a cabinet door. "You probably need the step stool to reach it." Billy let out a squawk, so Gran shifted him in her arms and stuck the nipple back into his open mouth.

Birdie ate her cereal to the accompaniment of his noisy sucking. At least somebody was happy.

"I didn't have time to make your lunch. Sorry. Do you mind buying today? There's change in that little jar over there. I forget what it costs."

"It's okay. I don't mind buying." Actually, life was a lot easier if she bought. But she didn't say that out loud.

She had hardly finished her cereal when the phone rang. It was Alicia, of course. "Where are you? You promised you wouldn't be late again."

She wanted to say that she'd never promised anything to anybody. Well, she had promised God, but that didn't matter anymore. Should she say her daddy was maybe this minute dying? Wouldn't that be enough to excuse everything? Somehow she couldn't. If she said something about Daddy, Alicia would probably claim her father was already dead, as if that won some kind of prize.

"I'm on the way," she said, and hung up.

"You don't have to go today, Elizabeth. Mr. Goldberg will understand if you want to stay home. Your mother will call us as soon as she . . ."

"No. I'll go." It would be harder just to sit here all day waiting for the phone to ring with bad news. She could put her mind on something else at school.

"Well, finally."

"Sorry." She was always apologizing to Alicia, but that was all the apology she could muster up this morning.

Alicia gabbled all the way to the schoolhouse. Birdie didn't bother to listen. They got there before the

125

eight-thirty bell, so at least Birdie didn't have to apologize again.

She slunk to her seat. She'd remembered to pick up her backpack from the hall floor, but it hadn't been opened. There was no completed homework to hand in. She always did her homework. What kind of excuse should she make up?

When the lunch bell rang, Mr. Goldberg asked her to wait a minute. She thought he was going to scold her; instead he said gently, "Are you okay, Elizabeth?" His voice was so kind, it made Birdie want to cry. "You don't look well. Would you like to go home?"

She pinched her lips together and nodded.

"Your grandmother called me about your dad. I'm so sorry. Would you like me to call her? She could come pick you up."

"No. I can walk."

"You're sure?"

She nodded.

"And you're sure your grandmother will be there? I don't want you going home to an empty house."

"She's always there."

"Okay. Get your things."

She collected her coat from the cloakroom and stuffed her books in her backpack.

"Just do yesterday's homework," he said before she could ask. "If you feel like it. You're a good student. You'll catch up."

She couldn't help it. She burst into tears. He was so kind. He came closer. He started to put his arm around her and stopped just in time, remembering the stupid no-hug rules. "Take care," he said. "I'll see you when you're feeling better."

She was never going to feel better. She knew that. But she only nodded and snuffled up the tears.

Birdie dropped her backpack and slipped out of her boots. "Elizabeth?"

"Yeah. It's me. Mr. Goldberg said I should come home."

"Good," Gran said. "Your mother called, and she wanted to talk to you as soon as you got home."

As Birdie stepped into the living room, Gran put down the book she had been reading on the little table beside her chair and got up. Birdie followed her back to the kitchen, where Gran picked up the phone and dialed a number. She handed it to Birdie.

There was nothing to do except take it and get whatever horrible news her mother was going to give her. In the end, it wasn't really any news at all. Mom was at some ratty hotel in DC. She hadn't seen Daddy. His plane wasn't even landing from Germany until tonight sometime, so, no, Mom didn't know anything yet. She told Birdie to pray again, and Birdie sighed into the phone and her mom took that for a promise.

Birdie asked Gran if she wanted to talk to Mom again before she hung up, so Gran took the phone and said goodbye and love and prayers and all those things you say when you don't know what to say and then hung up. "Well, that's that," she said. She looked at Birdie with a half smile, shook her head, and started back toward the living room

The baby monitor was on the table beside her chair. Gran glanced at it as she sat down. "I hope it's a long one," she said. "Neither of us got much sleep last night."

She turned to Birdie, still standing in the hall. "Can I help you, love? I know this is hard for you."

Birdie shook her head.

"Do you mind if I read?" Gran picked up the book, lying beside the baby monitor. "I seem to need something to occupy my mind." She bit her lip; her voice trembled. "He was such a beautiful little boy."

Oh, God! Was Gran going to cry? It was strange that Birdie hadn't thought of it. Daddy was Gran's baby. Nobody was thinking about how Gran was feeling right now. She was just worrying about everyone else. Birdie almost went over to her to . . . but what could she say? Those dumb things like *Don't worry. Everything will be all right.* When everything was certainly not going to be all right. Or worse: *I'm sorry for your loss*, when . . . but she couldn't think of that. And by the time she tried to think what to say, Gran had turned to her book and begun reading.

What was Birdie to do with the rest of the afternoon? She didn't feel like reading, and why write in her diary if she had nothing good to say in it? *I can't pray anymore because THERE IS NO GOD, or if there is a God, He's a mean liar and cheat and that's worse than not being at all.*

She should have stayed in school. She wasn't sick except in her heart, and you couldn't write an excuse note for something like that. She didn't tell Gran she hadn't had lunch. She'd save the money for another day. But weird as it was, she did feel hungry. At least, the hollow ache in her stomach might be hunger. How could you tell the difference?

She lay down on her bed, but she was wide awake. Maybe Gran was right.

Reading would take her mind off all the horrible thoughts fighting inside her head.

She reached for *The Diary of a Young Girl*. Anne's diary had been a book Daddy might have read. Funny he should have a book written by a girl when he was such a boy's boy. Maybe he'd read it at school. Or maybe, as Birdie had first thought, Gran had bought it.

Anne was smiling from the cover, which was ratty and wrinkled. It was a really old paperback. Last time she'd picked it up, the Franks had just gone into hiding in the Secret Annex. Anne had a lot of imagination; she'd probably do okay cooped up in an attic. Birdie liked that Anne was a real person—not that Birdie couldn't like fantasy anymore, now that there was no God to disapprove. But why was some kid, not that much older than Birdie herself, so famous that her diary got published? On the cover under Anne's picture, the *New York Times* said, "A truly remarkable book" and "to be read over and over for insight and enjoyment." Well, this book looked like it had been read over and over.

Birdie began flipping through the pages. Maybe the historical stuff at the end would explain why Anne was famous. She rolled over on her back and began to read. It was all about Germany and war and how the Nazis came to power and hated the Jews. (They would have hated Mr. Goldberg, too; he had said so himself.) It finally got to the part where the diary begins and starts to tell about how Anne and her sister, Margot, and their parents and the others started hiding in the secret apartment behind Mr. Frank's business. She knew all about that part.

Finally, the writer began telling about things past where Birdie had read. It told about the Nazi soldiers finding the hideout and—*oh, God*—taking everyone away to prison camp. Birdie didn't want to know what happened next, but she made herself go on. Anne had to stay alive. She had to! If Birdie kept reading, she could keep Anne alive.

"Margot died at the end of February or beginning of March, 1945. 'Anne, who was already sick at the time,' recalled a survivor, 'was not informed of her sister's death; but after a few days she sensed it, and soon afterwards she died, peacefully, feeling that nothing bad was happening to her.' She was not yet sixteen."

What a lie! Anne would not die peacefully. She knew good and well that something horrible was happening to her. Birdie sat straight up. She screamed and threw the wretched book across the room. It smashed against the wall. Yellowed pages fell out and scattered on the floor.

"Elizabeth!" Gran opened the door without knocking. She ran to the bed and put her arms around Birdie.

"She died!" Birdie cried. "They killed her!"

"Oh, my dear child," Gran said.

"It's not fair! All the good people die!"

Gran held her tight, and then they were both crying and crying and crying as though they could never stop.

And they might never have stopped except the phone began to ring. They both jumped up. Birdie got there first.

"Where the devil are you? You didn't even tell me you weren't coming to lunch! Who am I supposed to eat with? I swear. Sometimes I wonder why I gave up all my other friends for you."

She didn't want to talk to Alicia. Not today.

"Your little friend?" Gran asked.

"Yeah."

"Yeah, what?" Alicia was practically yelling through the phone. "Are you even listening to me? Now, get over here this minute! I do not want to have to walk all the way over there and drag you here. I swear. You're the one always begging to come over."

Birdie put her hand over the phone. "She wants me to come over."

"Do you want to?" Gran asked.

Birdie shrugged.

"Go ahead. We aren't going to get any news before tomorrow."

Alicia was sitting at the top of the porch stairs picking black polish off her nails. She looked up finally when Birdie started up the bottom stair. "Took you long enough."

"Sorry."

Alicia stood up. "Well, don't just stand there looking stupid. We got a lot to do today. You already wasted half our afternoon."

"Sorry," Birdie said again. It seemed to be the only word available. She didn't want to tell Alicia anything else. About Daddy. About Anne dying. About Gran crying like her heart was breaking. She was sure Alicia wouldn't help. Not that anyone could.

She followed Alicia into the house. "No Pop-Tarts for you today. Only get treats when you act right." No Pop-Tarts. That was a relief. Alicia wasn't whispering or tip-toeing, either, so her mom must be gone. Another relief.

Alicia had laid out a costume on her bed. It looked

like one of those Disney Princess dresses that Birdie'd begged for the Halloween when she was eight and never got because they cost too much. "Besides, they're tacky," her mom had said. "Really, Birdie, don't you think they're tacky?"

She had thought at the time that her mother was wrong, that the dress was beautiful. Looking at the dress laid out on the bed, she wondered whether, after all, Mom had been right.

"I'm trying to think about what shoes to wear with my Vegas costume. Don't worry. I don't expect you to help decide, but I thought you would want to know my thinking about style. I'm known for my sense of style."

Alicia cocked her head and stuck the tip of her tongue out through her narrow lips. "I'm thinking silver. It would pick up the silver here in the skirt. You see, Birdie, you need to think about the highlights you want emphasized. And a tiara. I'm thinking tiara."

Birdie was almost sure she knew what a tiara was, but she wasn't about to ask. What she wanted to ask was why Alicia needed her there at all. She should have stayed home with Gran. Gran might actually need her.

135

It was strange to think that Gran might need somebody else, especially her. Gran was the mother eagle. Birdie was the naked chick. Though right now, maybe, just maybe, they needed each other.

"You're not even listening! How are you ever going to learn about fashion if you don't pay attention?"

"Sorry."

"And that's another thing. I am sick to death of your 'sorry'! Just pay attention and do what you promise to do. Don't give me that wimpy 'sorry' every time you open your mouth!"

The front door opened but there was no sound of it shutting. There was noise, all right. It sounded like every pot in the kitchen was being thrown at the wall. "Alice May!"

Alicia slammed the door. "You've got to go home!" she hissed.

"Okay. Should I wait . . . ?"

"Mom and I . . . We need to discuss some . . ." Alicia was making it up as she went along, even Birdie could see that.

"I'll wait a minute before I go," she said.

"Yeah," said Alicia. "And tomorrow. Be on time for a change."

Birdie didn't bother to tiptoe. The cussing and swearing and hollering and banging of pots and pans from the kitchen would surely cover any possible noise Birdie might make on the stairs. She didn't know what was going on, but she knew she wanted out of that house. She started down the staircase.

Suddenly, the house went deadly quiet. Birdie froze. What should she do? Keep going down or race back to the bedroom? *He who hesitates is lost.* Birdie had no idea where that thought had come from or if it was true, but it must be, because there she was—this creature—roaring up the staircase to where Birdie stood. For a moment, Birdie thought the wild eyes had failed to see her standing there, but just as the woman came abreast, she turned her head and saw Birdie trembling there, her back against the wall. With a low animal snarl, she grabbed Birdie's right arm and twisted Birdie so that her anger-flushed face was inches from Birdie's ashen one.

"What the hell are you doing here?" The harsh

whisper was more frightening than the yelling had been. Claw-like fingernails bit into Birdie's flesh. She wanted to scream, but no sound, no words came out. It was like a nightmare when she couldn't speak or flee.

"Git!"

Birdie knew the spit-out word had landed on her cheek, but she didn't care. She wrenched free and ran down the stairs, almost tripping before she landed.

Racing past the kitchen, she might have heard someone moan, but it was soft, and Birdie couldn't go to help, anyway. She had to get away. Now.

She ran out the open front door, leaving it gaping wide behind her. She didn't stop running to zip up her jacket until she was a block down the street. Funny. She'd never even taken it off. It must have been cold in Alicia's room, and she hadn't even noticed.

Gran was sitting in her chair giving Billy yet another bottle. He was never going to learn to drink from a cup if Gran kept babying him. "Welcome back, sweetheart. I missed you." Gran realized Birdie was looking at the

138

bottle. She gave a little laugh. "Yes. I just don't have the strength to argue with him today."

"Well, he probably won't take a bottle to college," Birdie heard her own cracked voice say. It was the sort of joke Daddy might have made. Strange she could joke when her heart was beating like a drunken tom-tom. But she couldn't tell Gran what had just happened, not now, when Daddy was . . .

Gran shifted the baby in her arms. "Elizabeth, are you all right?"

"What do you mean?"

"I'm not sure. You look a little . . ."

"I'm fine. Just winded. I ran home."

"I see. And Alicia . . . Is everything all right over there?"

"Why wouldn't it be?"

"I don't know. It's just gossip, and I shouldn't repeat it, but I ran into one of their neighbors in the co-op and, well, she was worried," Gran explained.

"Worried?"

"There doesn't seem to be any father around, and

she said the neighbors are concerned that the child's mother . . . Well, Mrs. Marcioni saw a man . . ."

"Her dad's in the military," Birdie said quickly.

"Oh. And her mother . . . ?"

"There's nothing wrong with her mother." That was a monstrous lie. Why did she feel she had to defend Alicia's mother? And surely that woman on the stairs could only have been Alicia's mother.

"Well, I'm glad to hear it." Gran was carefully studying Birdie's face. "You'd tell me if . . . I mean, your mother trusts me to make sure—"

"Don't worry!" She wanted to get out of the room, but she made herself stand still and lower her voice. "Alicia's the only friend I got."

Gran nodded. "It takes time to make friends. I just hate for you to settle on just one person too quickly."

Birdie didn't want to talk about Alicia or friends anymore. She needed to think. She needed to be by herself. So she just nodded and went back into the hall to hang up her jacket. She liked the tall tree-like thing in the hall where you hung coats and umbrellas. It was hard to explain, but with its arms coming out from every side and on several levels, it felt so welcoming. Kind of like the Statue of Liberty. *Give me your poor, your tired, your Salvation Army jackets . . .* The coat tree didn't judge, just accepted anything you hung there. If only God were that kind. If He was at all.

She lay down on her bed. She hadn't made it up that morning. Mom had told Gran not to make up Birdie's bed. And Gran didn't. Birdie got off the lumpy covers and pulled them straight. Even if it wouldn't pass army inspection, as Daddy would say, it was smoother. *Oh, Daddy, why, why, why?*

She got down on her knees and pulled her diary out of the bottom drawer of the dresser. She needed to talk to someone. God wasn't listening, and Gran would ask too many questions. She took a nice sharp yellow pencil out of her pencil box and lay with her stomach down on the quilt and began to write furiously.

11
Are You There, God?

Dear Betsy Lou,

I'm writing you today because I really, truly need to talk to you. I guess I didn't tell you about Daddy. He's probably dying or maybe even dead by now. Grown-ups always say not to worry, everything will be all right, but I know it won't. Wasn't Gran crying her heart out? She didn't think everything was just fine. So why do grown-ups ever think they can fool kids? Then there's God. You are probably the only person

Was a diary a person? She couldn't call Betsy Lou a "thing." She was like a friend, and friends weren't things. Never mind—

only person who will understand my problem about God. Why I can't believe in Him anymore. We had this ~~bargain~~ promise. I would be a faithful believer in ~~H~~him and a faithful witness to Jesus, if God would keep Daddy safe. God did <u>not</u> keep his promise. Daddy is terribly wounded and is maybe going to die in some stupid hospital in Washington. I can tell by the way Mom and Gran stopped talking when I came in the room. You might think I don't love Daddy as much now that he loves Billy so much, but that is NOT TRUE. I love him more than ever even though he divided <u>his</u> love so I don't get as much of it as I used to. I don't care what Mom says that you just have more love for all your children, not less. That's just another grown-up lie. Love means giving a lot of attention. And who is getting ~~all~~ most of everybody's attention these days? You guessed it. Billy. And is he doing anything to deserve all that love? Is he being good and thoughtful and trying to help? Is he praying to God? Don't be silly. The more he screams and yells, the more attention he gets. I know. I know. He's only seven months old. But please don't say I'm acting like a baby and to GROW UP when I talk like this. I am ONLY HUMAN!!!! When I tried to be like Jesus who is supposed to be like really human but really God at the same time, it didn't work. I am not perfect like Jesus or God if there is a God, which I seriously doubt at this time. In fact, I think it's better not to have any God at all than one who acts all kind and good and like he's going to keep his promises one minute and then turns around and ruins your life, don't you?

Did I tell you God killed Anne Frank? Well, the Germans did, but God let them. Isn't that exactly the same thing? IF THERE IS A GOD, which as I said I am seriously doubting right now. And if there is no God there is no hell or heaven, either, for that matter. So it doesn't matter what you do. You could lie your head off. You could even hate your baby brother. You could probably just kill and murder people and it wouldn't matter one bit.

Birdie was holding the pencil so tightly and pressing so hard the point broke off. She felt hot all over. She sat up on the bed and pulled off her green sweater before she continued. Then she got up and got another pencil. This one had been sharpened so often it was only a stub with a bad point, but it would have to do for now.

Then there is the problem of my only friend besides you. Alicia. What do you think about Alicia? She does have a really scary mom, but does that excuse everything? I mean, I just don't like the way she tells me what I said when I really didn't say it. At least I can't remember saying it. Maybe I'm getting that thing old people get when they can't remember stuff. Does that ever happen to kids or is that just old people? Well, you know how Alicia orders me around all the time. I don't like that, either, but who would I eat lunch with or walk to school with or do things with after school if I didn't have Alicia for a kind of friend? And her mom . . . well, I think it was her mom. Who else could it be?

The phone was ringing. Not Alicia again. But she stopped trying to write and went and cracked the door.

Gran was talking softly, so it was hard to hear what she was saying, but, yes, Birdie was sure. Mom was on the phone. They didn't want her to know what was going on. Didn't she have a right to know? The only other phone was upstairs in Gran's bedroom. She tried to figure out how she could get to the stairs without Gran catching her. Was she going to spend all day sneaking up and down staircases? *Sheesh!* She opened the door just enough to slip out. The blinking thing creaked if you opened it too wide.

She tiptoed toward the staircase, but just before she got to the bottom step, she heard Gran say, "God bless you, darling. Call again when you can." So Birdie turned around and went toward the kitchen.

Gran was just hanging up when Birdie walked in. She sighed. "They let your mother see him at last. He's heavily sedated, and they're taking him in for more surgery."

If they were going to operate again, maybe everything would be all right after all. You didn't operate on almost-dead people, did you?

"So he's better?"

"I don't know. I'm sure they're doing everything they can." She gave a funny little shake of her head. "We've just got to keep praying, sweetheart."

Birdie nodded. It was a lie, but she didn't think it was the right time to tell Gran about God.

12
Secrets and Loss

Gran didn't wake Birdie up when Mom called that night to say Dad had survived the operation, but he was still not awake. *Heavily sedated* was the expression Gran kept using. Didn't that mean they conked you out with drugs? Why didn't they just say that?

Billy for once was not squawking. Gran had spread Cheerios on the high-chair tray, and he was happily picking them up one by one and putting them into his mouth and smiling every time as though he'd just climbed Mount Everest.

"Good boy!" Gran said. Honestly, was that all he had to do to get applause?

Birdie didn't want to go to school, and she was pretty sure Gran wouldn't make her go, but while she was still eating her oatmeal, the doorbell rang. Gran jumped a foot. *She thinks it's bad news, like soldiers coming to the door!* Neither of them moved, but it rang again, so Gran got up.

"Watch Billy, please, Elizabeth."

It was not soldiers. It was Alicia. She marched into the kitchen. "You still eating? Time to go."

Birdie looked at the kitchen clock. It wasn't even eight yet. She opened her mouth to say so but didn't.

"You've got plenty of time," Gran said. "More than an hour."

For once, Alicia didn't say anything, so Birdie felt she needed to explain. "Alicia likes to get there before the eight-thirty bell." Alicia said nothing to this. At least she didn't claim that getting there early was what Birdie said she wanted.

"Would you like some oatmeal?" Gran asked.

"No, I ate already."

Probably just a stinking Pop-Tart.

"Well, you could join us for a piece of toast, then." Gran pulled out Mom's chair.

"Oh. Okay." Alicia dropped her backpack and came

to the table. She was still wearing her pink jacket, and her blue boots were tracking water across the linoleum. She hadn't bothered to take her boots off at the door, even though there was a regular place right by the coat tree to leave them.

But what was that on her face? Alicia glared at her, so Birdie quickly dropped her gaze to her half-eaten oatmeal. But, really, it looked like the girl had plastered her face with makeup.

Nobody wore makeup to school. Well, some of the seventh and eighth graders wore a little lipstick, but real makeup? Not even the women teachers did that.

"Would you like a glass of milk?" Gran asked when she put the toast down.

Alicia wrinkled her nose. "You got coffee?"

Gran hesitated. "Well . . . yes." But she got a small mug and poured coffee into it. "A little milk, Alicia?"

"I guess."

Gran put some in. "There's sugar on the table." She put the mug down beside Alicia's plate of toast. She hesitated, waiting maybe for a thank-you. There wasn't one.

Birdie's mouth was half open to the prompt: *Say*

thank you. Hadn't her parents said that like a million times until it just became automatic? They had already started saying it to Billy, and he couldn't even talk.

But Alicia's head was already bent over the mug slurping the hot coffee. Then she jammed the toast into her mouth without putting down the cup. Maybe she hadn't even had a Pop-Tart. She looked like she was starving. The toast disappeared in a couple of bites.

Without asking, Gran put another piece of toast in front of Alicia. This one was slathered with peanut butter and a little grape jelly. Alicia didn't even grunt an acknowledgment. She just gobbled it down and handed the mug up to Gran with her mouth too full to speak.

Birdie noticed that this time there was more milk in the mug than actual coffee. She looked up at Gran across Alicia's bent head. Gran sent Birdie a quick eyebrow lift, as though to signal they both knew that Alicia had not already eaten earlier. "Okay." Alicia jumped up from the table. "We don't want to be late."

There was a lunch bag on the counter, so Gran had gotten up early enough to pack her a lunch, but Birdie pretended not to see it. "Don't worry about fixing me

151

lunch today, Gran. I got the money you gave me yesterday. I'll just buy today."

Gran looked puzzled, but, thankfully, she let it go.

When Birdie was pulling on her jacket and boots, Gran reappeared at the door. "You've been so kind to Birdie, Alicia. I'd love for you to join us at supper tonight."

"Um. Okay. If you want."

"Would you like for me to call your mother?"

"No!" Alicia's voice quickly returned to her mumble. "No, you don't need to call her. She won't mind. She's busy tonight anyway."

"Good. Then we'll look for you after school. We'll eat early. That way you can get home before it's completely dark."

"Okay." It wasn't okay with Birdie, but it couldn't be helped.

They missed the eight-thirty bell, but to Birdie's surprise, Alicia did not complain. They jostled in with the nine o'clock "losers." Several of the boys poked Birdie on their way past.

"Sorry," Wayne said. "Didn't mean to bump our little Tweeter."

All the boys laughed. She hated them all. Boys were horrible. Daddy was the only good boy in the world, and he . . . She mustn't even think about it.

No one brushed too close to Alicia. Maybe they'd learned better.

It wasn't a totally bad day. Birdie didn't feel too far behind in any of the subjects, and since she bought lunch, Alicia couldn't complain about that. She did mention that Birdie was once again wearing the green sweater. Hadn't she been reminded more than once that it made her look pasty? Now, Alicia, on the other hand, looked great in any color, but particularly in green. If Birdie ever wised up and got rid of that sweater, she should let Alicia try it on first—just to show Birdie how good it would look on someone with Alicia's complexion. But why, then, was Alicia's "flawless" complexion covered up with makeup? Birdie didn't ask.

In the middle of Mr. Goldberg's read-aloud time, Birdie suddenly sat up straight. What was the matter with her? Daddy might be dying right this minute and she'd hardly thought of him all day long. She began to breathe funny. Maybe that's how you felt when someone close to you stopped breathing. *Oh, God, if you're there . . .*

Mr. Goldberg asked her to stay a minute after the dismissal bell. She sat in her seat while almost every boy in the class—even boys at tables across the room—somehow wound their way past her chair and, checking to make sure Mr. Goldberg wasn't looking, hit one of her arms on their way toward the door. Alicia, too, stopped at her table on the way out and gave her that look that meant she'd be waiting outside, and Birdie'd better not be late again.

"Thank you for waiting, Birdie." Oh, God, he was using her nickname. It had to be bad news.

"My daddy!" She couldn't help blurting it out.

"No, no," he said. He pulled up a chair close to hers. "Oh, dear, I'm sorry to alarm you. It's not your father. It's Alice—uh—Alicia."

"Alicia?" *What about Alicia?*

"Well, you seem to be spending a lot of time with her."

What of it? She's the only one who wants to my friend.

"You must have noticed that when she came to school this morning, she was wearing a lot of makeup. And not for the first time. You see . . ."

He hesitated before he continued. "I'm worried about her. I've tried to contact her parents. I've left a number of messages on the phone, but neither parent calls back."

"Her dad's in the service?" She heard her own voice rise into a question mark.

"You got that from Alice, I take it." He pressed his lips together. "What about her mother? Have you ever met her mother?"

Did that scene on the staircase count as *meeting* Alicia's mom?

He was tracing his index finger in the grooves in the tabletop that spelled out *WAYNE*. "I can't," Mr. Goldberg said at last, "I can't discuss any matters like this with a student, but you could tell your grandmother if—" He stopped abruptly. "Maybe both of us should talk with your grandmother." He gave her a crooked smile. "Now you'd better go on. I'm sure Alice is waiting for you." The strange smile was twisting his nice full lips into a thin line. "She doesn't need to know what we've discussed."

155

At her cubby, she began to understand what it was that Mr. Goldberg was *not* saying. He thought Alicia's mother was hurting her. There were all those yells and the strange sounds. But as much as Mrs. Suggs scared her, Birdie had never actually *seen* her hit Alicia. She stuffed her backpack with too many books and hurried to the door.

Mr. Goldberg was holding it open for her.

"Don't worry," she said to his very worried face. "I won't say anything to Alicia."

"Thanks," he said.

"Wake up!" The bonk on her head brought her wide awake. "Good God. I been waiting out here for hours. Do you think I got nothing better to do than stand here in the freezing cold until you decide to mosey out?"

"Sorry."

"What did Goldberg want, anyway?"

Mr. Goldberg. *Mr.* Goldberg. "Oh, you know, he wanted to say he was thinking about me."

"About you? What for?"

"My dad. Didn't I tell you he . . ."

"He's only a corporal. Not like he was a full colonel in the regular air force where it's actually dangerous."

Birdie could feel the prickle rising in her body. Daddy might be actually dying, and . . . but she pinched her lips together. It was none of Alicia's business. She'd only take the fact that Birdie's daddy was probably dying and squash it into nothing.

"When we get to your house, the first thing you should do is take off that sweater. I know you got a pink one that doesn't look too bad. Then, like you said, I should try on the green one. You need to see how much better it looks on someone with the right complexion."

Yeah. Someone wearing so much freaking makeup you can't see her face at all.

Sometimes Birdie wondered how she put up with Alicia. And then she felt ashamed. Even if she didn't believe in God hardly at all, Bible verses kept popping into her head. "Be ye kind, one to another," for one. It was good to be kind. And even if God wasn't telling her what to do anymore, Daddy was so kind. He'd want her to be kind. And besides, she didn't have anybody else to hang around with. She would be totally alone if

157

it weren't for Alicia. Mr. Goldberg had said she should talk to Gran about Alicia. But if she did, if she told Gran about all the pounding and yelling and moaning and Mrs. Suggs meeting her on the stairs, what would happen to Alicia? They'd probably send her away to a terrible foster home or reform school or orphanage or wherever they sent kids whose parents beat up on them. As mad as she was at Alicia, she couldn't do that to her.

A jab on her arm. "Oww."

"Well, pay attention, then. I'm discussing whether I should order the silver strap sandals from the internet or get Mom to take me shopping in Burlington for them. They probably have a half-decent shoe store in Burlington, not that you'd know."

Birdie didn't want Alicia to come home with her even though Gran had invited her. She didn't want to walk into the house and have Alicia standing there when Birdie heard news about Daddy, but Alicia was practically hanging on her arm as they went up the steps. Could she say, *Go away, Alicia*? If she'd even wanted to, there wasn't a teeny-weeny hole in Alicia's endless wall of sentences to poke a word through.

"I'm home!" Birdie was yelling, she knew she was, but she was trying to warn Gran not to say anything with Alicia there. Gran must have leaped from her chair, because she was already standing in the hall facing the door when the girls pushed through. She shook her head slightly when she realized Alicia was right behind Birdie.

"Oh, Alicia," she said. "I'm afraid I totally forgot you were coming. This is not a good time. I'll have to renege on my supper invitation."

Alicia looked up, confused. "What?"

"I can't ask you to stay for supper tonight. It's a family concern. I'm so sorry, dear."

A chill went through Birdie's body. Alicia hadn't moved. It seemed to Birdie that she'd never move. How could Birdie get rid of her? She could think of only one way. She ripped off her jacket and her green sweater.

"Here," she said, holding the sweater out toward Alicia. "Try it on at your house. You've got the best mirror."

"Okay." Alicia snatched the sweater. She looked like some homeless person grabbing a burger. "Okay. See you tomorrow."

"You may join us for breakfast if you like," Gran said. *Oh cripes.* Gran was kinder than the Bible.

"Okay. If you want." Alicia was practically hugging Birdie's sweater to her heart.

Gran waited without speaking, but as soon as the door slammed closed, Birdie blurted out, "He's dead."

"No, no, sweetheart." Gran put her arm around Birdie and pulled her close. She wasn't crying, so maybe . . .

"He's not awake yet, but your mom has seen him again, and she feels better. Some of the shrapnel hit his face"—Birdie felt a chill before Gran went on—"but the—the doctors have removed it, and they don't believe his brain has been injured. Which is a mercy. But . . ." She took a breath. "He may lose one or perhaps both of his legs."

"His legs?"

"Yes," said Gran. "His legs." Here her breath turned into a sigh. "We'll just have to wait and see what they decide."

But he wouldn't be able to walk or run or really play sports ever again.

"Oh, sweetheart, they're doing wonderful things with artificial limbs these days." Gran was reading her mind again. "We can't give up hope at this point." She hugged Birdie tighter. "He's alive. He'll still have his bright, wonderful mind . . ."

"It's all my fault."

"What? None of this is your fault, Elizabeth! How in the world—?"

"I didn't pray right. I—"

"Oh, baby, there's no wrong way to pray. And right now, I think the best way to pray is just to cry. I know God is crying."

It was a crazy idea. God crying. But still, as they held each other, it felt so good to be held tightly and to cry. She put her own arms around Gran's small waist and laid her head against Gran's thin bosom and cried and cried some more. So even if there wasn't a God who cared, much less cried, Gran was the next best thing.

13
Bleeding Heart

Birdie had decided not to get up, maybe ever again, so she was still lying in bed when the doorbell began to ring. She rolled over onto her back, listening to the quiet mumble of Gran's voice as she tried to poke Billy's breakfast into him, now rudely punctuated by the repeated *br-iiing* of the bell.

"Could you get that for me, Elizabeth?"

God! Not more bad news, please! But she got up, threw on her bathrobe, and pattered to the door in her bare feet.

Alicia! It wasn't even daylight yet, and there she stood, demanding to be let in. "Jesus! Do you know how long I been out here in the cold waiting for you to open the freaking door? You're the one who said I had to come for breakfast like I was your some kinda nursemaid." She pitched her pink jacket in the corner of the hall, revealing the green sweater underneath, and marched her wet blue boots into the kitchen.

"Good morning, Alicia. You're here bright and early."

Alicia ducked her head and mumbled. "I didn't want us to be late. For school."

"No," said Gran. "Of course not." She had turned her full attention from Billy's locked-up mouth to Alicia. "Have a seat, dear. As soon as I finish feeding the baby, I'll get you girls some breakfast." She turned back toward Billy and opened her own mouth to try to encourage Billy to open his. After a semisuccessful spoonful, she wiped his face with his bib and without turning around said in a mild tone of voice, "I see you're wearing Elizabeth's sweater today."

"She wants me to." It was the mumbly voice Alicia seemed to take with Gran.

"I see. Well, I guess that's between you girls. Anyhow, I know Elizabeth won't be wearing it today.

Ah, we should have called you. Elizabeth isn't going to school today."

I'm not? It wasn't as if she wanted to, but she was surprised Gran hadn't given her a choice.

"She don't look sick to me," Alicia mumbled.

"She's not. I need her here today. I'll call the school and explain."

"Okay. Whatever."

The breakfast, when it came, was lavish. Scrambled eggs with cheese mixed in, sausage, buttered toast with a choice of jams and jellies. Orange juice for each of them. A tall glass of milk for Birdie and a mug of hot milk for Alicia, colored tan with coffee.

Alicia didn't even nod a thank-you, just dived in and attacked her plate like a starving hyena.

Birdie would have sworn that she couldn't eat, but she realized suddenly that she had already taken several bites of egg and chewed and swallowed them without tasting. She forced herself to slow down. She didn't want Gran to see her eating like Alicia. And, oh, despite everything, it tasted good. Birdie chose the strawberry jam because she and Daddy had picked strawberries together last June. Was it before or after Billy was born? It must have been before, but she couldn't remember. She did remember the warm early-summer sun and all the laughter, not about anything, really, just laughing because they had so much fun being together, just the two of them.

Birdie was so wrapped up in her own thoughts, she hardly noticed when Alicia left for school. Had she said goodbye? Well she sure hadn't said thank you. No matter how zonked out Birdie was, she certainly would have heard if Alicia had said that. And neither Birdie nor Gran had said anything about Alicia's caked-on makeup, not aloud, anyway.

Breakfast was over, and she couldn't just sit at the kitchen table forever. She supposed she ought to put some clothes on. She wandered back into her room. It didn't matter what she put on. Alicia had her green sweater, which was the only thing she really liked. Her Jesus shirt was hanging on one of her clothes hooks. She didn't sleep in it or wear it under things now that she'd pretty much stopped believing. It seemed like a lie. But how could you know what was true and what was real? She put it on, just in case . . . and pulled an old sweater on top. It was the "not too bad" pink one that was worn to the point where there were little pink pills all over it, but she wasn't going anywhere. No one would make fun of it.

When the phone rang, she jumped off her bed and ran into the sitting room. Gran was already there, nodding into the phone. She turned toward Birdie and mouthed *okay*. "Your mom wants to speak with you," she said, handing the phone to Birdie.

"Mom?"

"I don't want you to worry, sweetie—" How could she not worry? "They're taking Dad into surgery this afternoon."

"What?"

"I don't want you to get upset, sweetheart. Everything's going to be all right."

"What do you mean *all right*?"

"They are going to amputate—"

"Amputate!"

"Shh, sweetie. It's all right. I mean, it's going to be all right. I promise. He's a trouper. He's alive. We need to be thankful—"

But Birdie could hear the tears wrapped around every word. Who needed to be thankful? She certainly wasn't. What kind of God would play such a cruel trick on somebody as good as her daddy?

"Are you still there?"

"Yeah." She didn't even try to hide the anger in her own voice. "What did Daddy say?"

"Well, he's not really awake right now."

"They're going to chop off his leg without even telling him?"

"The surgeon explained and—"

"They are, aren't they? You gotta stop them!"

"Oh, Birdie, I'm so sorry. I know it's hard to understand—"

"You're on their side!"

"Birdie—"

"Here!" She jammed the phone into Gran's stomach and went back to her room. She slammed the door, and, because it didn't make quite enough noise, she opened and slammed it again to make sure Mom could hear it through the phone wires.

But it wasn't enough. She had to do something or

167

go somewhere or her insides would explode. What if your insides really did explode? That would kill you, all right. Then you wouldn't have to live in a terrible world where good people went to war and parts of them really got exploded like Daddy's had. Dead people didn't have to even think about horrible things like that.

But Birdie didn't want to die. She didn't know what happened to people when they died. Didn't Counselor Ron say that people who didn't believe right went to hell when they died? She didn't believe in God anymore or Jesus, either, so maybe there was no hell. But how could you be sure?

She rammed her bottom down on the bed. She pulled off her sweater and threw it to the foot of the bed. Her I ❤ JESUS shirt underneath felt sticky and gross. She balled it up and hurled it under the bed. She couldn't figure anything out. Everything was too hard.

She had to stop thinking. If she didn't, she would only think about Daddy getting his leg chopped off—or did they saw it off? Oh, God, she couldn't think about that! And she couldn't think about going to hell. What could she think about? She pulled the pink sweater on over her bare chest and got up and opened the door. Gran was off the phone and nowhere to be seen. She must be upstairs with Billy. Birdie ran out into the hall. "I'm going to school!"

Mr. Goldberg looked up with surprise when she came into the classroom. "Oh, hi," he said. "Your grand-mother called to say you weren't coming today." And, just as Birdie passed his desk, he said, so quietly that no one else could hear, "I know you all must be terribly anxious."

She nodded and tried to smile before she went into the cloakroom, shed her jacket, and took her books and supplies out of her backpack. She stood still for a while, just breathing, before she made her way to her seat at the table.

Wayne leaned over to Devon and whispered some-thing, his eyes on Birdie's face, so she knew he was talking about her.

"Mr. Crenshaw"—Wayne sat up a bit straighter— "would you kindly pay attention to the task at hand?" Mr. Goldberg said.

Wayne was still smirking, but he lowered his eyes to the math worksheet in front of him.

Mr. Goldberg brought a sheet for Birdie. When she looked down at it, it made no sense. It was like math had suddenly turned into ancient Egyptian or something. She didn't even open her pencil box. He stood there for a minute looking at her. "Are you all right, Birdie?"

Wayne gave a snort. Devon covered his mouth to stifle a giggle. "Gentlemen. Would the two of you please go stand in the hall until you can pull yourselves together?"

Wayne and Devon pushed back from the table, scraping the floor so hard it sounded like the screech of the brakes on a semi. When Wayne stood up, his chair banged backward onto the floor.

Mr. Goldberg watched and waited until Wayne finally picked up the chair and shoved it to the table. The room was deathly still as the two boys marched into the hall and shut the door behind them. Birdie could hear their nervous giggles through the heavy wood.

"Now," he said, turning to Birdie. "I think you may have a little catching up to do. Why don't you bring your chair up to my desk and let's see what's what."

She stood up and picked up the math sheet. When she turned to get her chair, she caught a glimpse of Alicia staring at her. Alicia was, of course, still wearing the green sweater, but now it was the heavy makeup that made Birdie stare back. And in that one glance it all made sense. All the lies. All the things that Alicia had tried to make her believe were not only good but absolutely amazing and fantastic. There wasn't any "sister act." There wasn't any gig. Certainly no Las Vegas. *Alice May!* There wasn't even any Alicia Marie. There was just poor stupid Alice May, whose awful mother cussed and yelled and probably beat her. And Birdie had believed all the lies—or tried to. Here she, Birdie, was trying to be kind and protect Alicia— Alicia who acted like Birdie's brave daddy was nothing while her own invented daddy was some big shot with medals. How could she have been so stupid for so long?

So when Mr. Goldberg dismissed the class for lunch, she hung back until the room emptied. She waited until he closed the door and came back to his desk. "Was there something you wanted to ask me, Elizabeth?"

171

"It's true. Her mom beats her."

He bent down so he was looking her straight in the face. "You've actually witnessed—"

"Yeah. I mean, yessir. It's bad. Ask my gran."

"Thank you, Birdie. I will." He started for the door. When she didn't follow him, he turned around. "It's time for lunch. Do you need to get yours from the cloakroom?"

"I don't feel so good."

"I'll call your grandmother to let her know you're on the way home, shall I?"

"Yeah. Yessir. Thank you."

Somehow, miraculously, Alicia was not waiting at the door. Birdie walked as fast as she could down the hall. She didn't want any of those bossy hall monitors stopping her for running, but once out the heavy front door she began to accelerate, and long before she reached the final corner, she ran like demons were chasing her. She skidded once on a patch of ice but caught herself before she fell. Freaking town! Nothing was safe here. Nothing was safe anywhere.

When she opened the front door, she could hear Gran talking on the phone in an official voice. She wasn't talking to Mom, then. It was either Mr. Goldberg or maybe even the police. Yeah, the police. That would be good.

Birdie slipped her boots and jacket off and tiptoed to her bedroom in her sock feet. The door squeaked, of course, but she closed it as quietly as she could. Still, Gran must have heard because, within seconds, there was a knock on her door.

Even though she said nothing, Gran opened the door. "That was Mr. Goldberg."

"Yeah?"

"Two things. He's worried about you." Gran paused, coming closer to the bed where Birdie was still sitting, stiff as ice. "And . . ." Here she sighed and sat down beside Birdie. "He asked about Alicia."

"What about her?"

"He wanted to know if I had any indication that she was being abused at home."

"Yeah?"

"Mr. Goldberg said you had witnessed it."

Well, she had, hadn't she? Practically seen it with her own eyes. Certainly heard it.

Maybe it was the thought of that crazy face so close to her own and the fingernails pressing into her wrist that made her say, "Yeah. I saw it. Her mom beats her."

"I feared as much. All that makeup."

Birdie slid her legs up onto the bed and turned her back to Gran. "They oughta send her to jail." Her muttering didn't indicate who should go to jail. She didn't care. Mrs. Suggs? Alicia? Maybe they both should. Anybody who lied and stole like Alicia—

"Mr. Goldberg wants to be absolutely sure before either of us calls social services. He made a terrible mistake a few years ago and, well, he never wants to do that again . . . So you're sure . . ."

"Yeah. I'm sure."

She wouldn't take the phone when Mom called, even when Gran brought it to her on the bed. She didn't want to hear about Daddy—his leg chopped off and bleeding. His mind so muddled up that he couldn't even say he didn't want it to happen. Of course he didn't want it to happen! They didn't know Daddy at all if they thought for one freaking minute he'd want anything that horrible! She stuck her pillow in her mouth so she wouldn't scream out loud.

And then she heard the little voice in her head. *It's all your fault, you know.*

She sat up straight. How could this awfulness be all her fault? It was all God's fault! She'd tried to keep her side of the bargain. Bargain. Ha! You can't bargain with a liar and a cheat. Alicia had taught her that much. She banged the pillow down on the bed. It wasn't enough. So she threw it hard—the length of the narrow room. It hit the door and fell soundlessly to the floor. Not even a little whoosh of complaint.

She was crying. She shouldn't be crying. She wasn't sad; she was furious! Where was that freaking T-shirt? **I ♥ JESUS**. She hated Jesus. He was supposed to make God be on her side, if there was a God, and there probably was. No human being could make such a mess of the entire world!

She got on her knees and looked under the bed. It was dark, but she thought she could see it there against the wall. It was just out of reach. She lay down on her belly to slither toward it. It was dusty, and her nose twitched as though she might sneeze. She reached the shirt with her fingers and pulled and wriggled back. When she stood up, she could see how dirty it had become. When did Gran vacuum? *Sheesh.* She couldn't have guessed the floor under the bed would be that dirty. The shirt was a mess.

She felt a pang of something like sympathy toward it. No! It was God who had flunked, not the shirt. Even if she was going to throw it away—and she was certainly going to throw it away or at best give it to Salvation Army for some other fool kid to wear—it ought to be cleaner.

She took it into the little half bath and filled the sink with hot water. She couldn't remember if the shirt had ever been washed before. Probably not. Earlier she hadn't ever wanted to take it off. She plunged it into the hot water, but when she reached for the bar of soap, she realized that there was something in the water. She turned toward the door and switched on the light. Pink. The water was pink. The bright red heart was bleeding right into the wash water. She pulled the shirt out, but it was too late. The water had turned pink. It was like the heart was crying.

She started to cry again. God is crying. She wrung out the pink water and hung the ruined shirt over the radiator, which hissed in protest.

"Elizabeth?" Gran was off the phone at last. "Are you all right?"

How in the devil was she supposed to answer that? She didn't, which meant Gran was headed her way. She didn't want Gran to see the shirt. She jumped out of the bathroom and waited in front of the closed door.

"Are you all right, dear?"

"Yeah. I'm okay."

"I've spoken to Child Welfare."

"Yeah?" Mom would have corrected her, but Gran didn't.

"They'll take Alicia to someplace safe. You mustn't worry."

"Okay." Birdie turned away. If Gran said another word, she might scream.

She needed to get away, back to her room where

she could shut the door, but Gran was on her heels. "Your mom called earlier. The surgery was successful. She doesn't want you—" But here, Gran stopped. Even without turning around, Birdie knew she was crying. *My beautiful boy,* Gran had said. Her baby.

Birdie couldn't stand it. She turned and reached out her arms, and Gran came to her as though Birdie were the grown-up and she the child. "Jesus is crying, too," Birdie said. That was the verse. The shortest verse in the Bible. Reverend Colston wouldn't let them use it to answer Bible roll call because it was only two words long and everyone could memorize it without even trying. "Jesus wept." It was in the Bible. And if Jesus could cry, so could God. And so could Gran and so could Birdie and so could the whole bleeding world.

When the phone rang, Birdie answered it.

"They even let criminals have one phone call," Alicia said.

"Where are you?" Birdie asked.

"I don't know. They picked me up at school."

There was a pause. "You were the one ratted me out. So don't lie."

"She does beat you, doesn't she?" Birdie tried to force her voice to sound strong.

"That's none of your freaking business."

"I'm sorry, Alicia."

"You're sorry, all right. Some sorry excuse for a friend."

"Maybe things will be better for you."

"Yeah? You think? With my mom in jail and me going to some rotten foster place?"

"In jail?" Birdie's voice had become tiny again.

"She only takes that stuff to be strong for her act. And she hardly ever sells it."

"Oh."

"Well, have a nice life, Judas." Birdie heard the sound of a phone crashing into its base and then the humming of a broken connection.

She stood there amazed, not at Alicia's anger so much as that the girl knew who Judas was. The hum seemed to grow louder, so she pressed the off button on her own phone. The button had a little red telephone on it. Red was like stop or blood. Oh, God. What a mess she'd made of everything. She *was* like Judas who betrayed Jesus. Alicia was no Jesus, but then . . .

She remembered when Reverend Colston had read them the judgment scene where Jesus says to everyone before his throne that whenever you are not kind to people in need or to strangers, you are not being kind to him. So you had to be kind to the "least of these," who are Jesus's brothers and sisters, or God wouldn't be kind to you. Would God or Jesus send her away to hell because, instead of being kind, she had betrayed Alicia?

Even if God forgave her, Alicia never would, if—and that was a big if—*if* she even saw her again. Her daddy would say, if he could say anything, that it was not her fault, but God would know. God knew everything.

The longest day of her life turned into the longest week. Another morning came and then another. The store called to ask where Mom was, and they were sorry, but the headquarters didn't give "compassionate leave," and she hadn't worked long enough for sick days or vacation or even to hold her job. When she got back she could, of course, reapply . . .

At school Birdie stayed to herself. She took her lunch every day, but she didn't try to sit with anyone. Christie and her crowd had given up on her ages ago, and she wanted to sit as far away from Wayne and his gang as possible. Once she took a library book and pretended to read while she ate, but the teacher on duty made her quit. She might drop something on the book. So she just stared at her sandwich without bothering to taste and chewed each bite slowly and deliberately. Sometimes she counted the chews before she swallowed, but much past sixty, there wasn't anything left to chew.

The only good thing about school was the last twenty minutes, when Mr. Goldberg read out loud. She could see, though, that the pages to the end of the book were getting fewer and fewer, and then that one good thing would be over.

Friday afternoon, Mr. Goldberg asked her to wait after school so he could speak with her.

She stayed in her seat and laid her head down on the table. She ignored the punches and snide whispers of Wayne and his gang as they went out of their way to thwack her arm or scrape a hand across her hair.

Mr. Goldberg came in from the hall and closed the door after himself. He walked over to the desk and picked up a small book before he came over to Birdie's table, pulled out a chair, and sat down beside her.

"This has been a terrible time, hasn't it?"

Birdie lifted her head off the table and looked at him. The hair on top of his head was thinning, but underneath, his face was so kind, she was afraid it would make her cry.

"Your father—then Alice—"

Birdie bit the inside of her cheek and nodded.

"We adults have managed to make a mess of this beautiful world, haven't we?" Did Mr. Goldberg—kind, wise Mr. Goldberg—think everything was his fault?

She looked into his sad eyes. He seemed to.

"I know you like *The Tale of Despereaux*, so I checked another of Kate DiCamillo's books out for you. I think it's the first one she wrote, but I really like it, and I thought you might, too." He pushed the small, fat book toward her. "Sometimes, when life seems particularly hard, I just like to lose myself in a good book, don't you?" It was something Gran might say.

She nodded again, then reached out and ran her fingers over the title. *Because of Winn-Dixie.* There was a girl and a dog in the picture. Birdie's old apartment hadn't allowed pets. Daddy used to talk about the dogs he'd had growing up. They were like brothers and sisters to him, so he didn't mind being an only child. When his own daddy died, he still had Abner. "You have no idea what a comfort a dog is," he'd said once, his voice full of longing. Abner died the first year after he and Mom got married. Gran was gone all day teaching, so she didn't get another dog. She should have, though. She needed one.

Mr. Goldberg patted her arm. "Okay?"

She nodded.

"See you Monday. Take care."

She nodded again before she stood up and started for the cloakroom.

"I hope things will soon get better for all of you," he said. He didn't say, *Everything will be all right.* He knew better than try to lie to a kid.

Opal's mom had run away from home when Opal was a baby. Opal couldn't even remember her, and Opal's daddy didn't talk about her mom. That was sad for Opal, but she had a really nice daddy otherwise. He was a preacher. Not an old one like Reverend Colston or someone like Counselor Ron who was always talking about hell, but one more like Daddy or Mr. Goldberg—gentle and kind. Still, life was hard for Opal. She was lonely, even with having a good daddy. Things got better for Opal in the book because of Winn-Dixie. He was a stray dog Opal met in the Winn-Dixie grocery store. Which is a strange name for a grocery store. But that's why Opal named the dog Winn-Dixie. Having a dog was like a miracle for Opal.

Birdie really needed to talk with Gran about getting a dog. Not Mom. Mom would say a dog would be too much trouble for Gran when she had both Billy and Birdie to take care of already. But Gran had once had dogs. She would know that people, especially lonely kids, needed a dog. And Daddy, too. Daddy thought dogs were such a comfort. He'd said that. And he would really need a dog now, wouldn't he? He had lost so much. A dog would give him comfort, help him get better. She was sure it would.

The phone was ringing. She stopped reading in the middle of a sentence. Keeping her finger in as a book-mark, she went to the door and opened it. Yes, Gran was talking to Mom. Somehow Opal and Winn-Dixie had made her feel braver.

She went into the kitchen.

Gran turned. "Hold on a minute, Susan. There's someone here who wants to talk with you." Birdie swapped her book with the phone Gran was holding out, and Gran stuck her own pointer finger into the pages to hold Birdie's place.

"Mom?"

"Hi, darling. How are you?"

"Okay. When are you and Daddy coming back?"

"I'm not sure."

"Oh."

"That's why I thought you might want to come down here for a visit."

"Really?" It seemed too much to hope for.

"There's a direct flight from Burlington, and I'd be right there to meet you . . ."

"I'm not scared." It was a lie, but she needed to say it.

"Good."

Mom hadn't said anything about how much it cost, and she didn't even have a job anymore. Maybe she didn't know about the job yet, but still . . .

"Gran wants you to have it for an early birthday present." So they'd already discussed it.

"Okay. When?"

"As soon as we can arrange things, sweetie. Maybe next week at the earliest."

Next week sounded like forever, but still, it was sometime. She had to see Daddy, or what was left of him. Oh, God! Supposed she freaked out when she saw him all crippled and messed up? Maybe she shouldn't go. Maybe if he saw her and she was all funny, he might get worse. Or just give up.

"Birdie? Are you still there?"

"Yeah."

"I thought you wanted to come."

"I do. Really. It's just—"

"I know, sweetie. But it will be all right."

There she went, talking like a grown-up. "Yeah. Okay. Well—"

"Bye, sweetie. I love you."

"Me too."

"Keep up those good prayers."

"Yeah. Well. Bye." She handed the phone back to Gran, who was looking at her. Puzzled? Sad? It was hard to tell. Anyhow, she took the phone from Birdie's outstretched hand and turned toward the window.

Birdie didn't wait to hear what Gran was saying to Mom. Birdie's book was on the kitchen table. Gran had stuck in a torn-off bit of the grocery list tablet for a bookmark. Birdie picked it up and headed for her room. But before she began reading again and forgot to do it, she went to check on the Jesus shirt. It was now dry. She took it off the radiator and turned it over to the other side. With the shirt backside up, she didn't see the bleeding heart anymore, but even the back was splotchy from the dye that had run into the water.

I'm sorry. It's not your fault. She wasn't sure who she was talking to. Jesus, maybe?

14
Forgive Our Trespasses

The airlines were knocking themselves out to be good to "our heroes." They didn't lower the price of the ticket actually, but they let Gran get a ticket for the following Saturday for the same price as if she'd booked three or more weeks in advance. Gran sort of snorted when she was telling Birdie about the exchange. "They were so almighty proud of themselves! You'd think they'd offered to send you first class on a private jet."

So Birdie was really going. She had to get herself ready. She wasn't sure she was truly back to believing right, but she would begin to pray anyway. It was like life insurance. Just in case there really was a good God and He had sent Jesus to save Birdie from all her sins. When she took her Jesus shirt off the radiator, it was stiff as a board. She rolled it up to try to soften it, but it still felt scratchy on her bare skin. Never mind. It would loosen up. It was ugly now, but when she wore it under things, no one would see that she had ruined it.

She lay awake for a long time that night. Her Jesus shirt was under her pajama top. She wanted to start praying again, but she had trouble remembering how to do it the right way. Gran had said there was no wrong way, but, *Sorry, Gran, you are wrong about that.* It probably comes from being a Congregationalist. Counselor Ron had warned them about liberal Christians like Congregationalists.

Our Father, who art in heaven . . . Was God like a daddy, like her kind daddy, or was he more like the guy Counselor Ron talked about, like some really strict guy who had his eye out for everything you did wrong? Like someone who made Jesus die because somebody had to be punished for how awful everyone on earth was, from Adam all the way to her, Birdie, who didn't pray right, didn't believe right, failed her own daddy, and betrayed her best, well, her only friend?

She could still hear Alicia's voice full of anger and

something more than anger. *Have a nice life, Judas.* Was it hurt? Had Birdie wounded Alicia? *And forgive us our trespasses—* She had asked Daddy on the walk home from church one Sunday what "trespasses" were. "Is it like you ran all over somebody else's backyard?" That didn't make good sense.

Daddy had laughed. "No," he'd said. "It means asking God to forgive the things you have done wrong. But that's the first half. The second half says 'Just like we forgive those who do bad things to us.'"

"Huh?"

Daddy had smiled and squeezed her hand. "God doesn't want us just to love him; he wants us to love each other. And that means forgiving someone who hurts us."

"Oh," she had said, as though she understood when she really hadn't.

But now, there was Jesus, whom she might really have hurt, and Alicia, who had lied to her and kept her from having other friends and was blaming her for everything. Well, Alicia had her favorite sweater. Not that Birdie had given it to her. "God loveth a cheerful giver." She sure wasn't cheerful about it, but she hadn't tried to snatch it back. Maybe that sort of counted as forgiving Alicia for stealing it. *Well, God, you can't have everything!* Birdie smiled despite herself.

Maybe God thought it was funny, too. You never knew about God.

She got through the week on all kinds of funny prayer and reading Opal's story five times.

Next to dogs, books were the best comfort. And if the dogs were only in stories or imaginary, books won.

On Saturday one of Gran's friends came to babysit Billy so Gran could take Birdie to the plane. He began to cry as soon as Gran put him in Mrs. Shelton's arms. He reached his chubby arms out for Gran to take him back. Birdie's heart gave a little twist. Poor baby. He knew awful things were happening, but he couldn't understand them. Impulsively, she went over and took his hand and kissed it. "There, there," she said. "Don't cry, Billy Boy. Everything is gonna be all right."

She was sitting in her seat on the plane before she'd realized that she'd spoken like a stupid grown-up to her poor little brother.

15

The Rainbow Halo

The airline people wouldn't let Gran go past security, but they let Birdie get on the plane just after an old man in a wheelchair. The attendant helped Birdie find her seat and buckled her in. "You're lucky to have a window seat," she said. "It's a beautiful day." She put Birdie's jacket and the little suitcase Gran had loaned her into the overhead compartment. "I'll help you get these down when we land, don't worry. Just sit back and enjoy the view."

Birdie wasn't sure how enjoyable that would be. She didn't even like to climb trees and look down. It would be scarier in an airplane to look down all that way.

Before too long other people began to pile onto

the plane. She hoped no one would sit next to her. She wouldn't know what to say to a stranger. You really shouldn't talk to strangers anyway. Good. Everyone was going somewhere else. But as soon as she thought that, a tall skinny man and a big round woman stopped right beside her seat. The man pushed Gran's suitcase and Birdie's jacket aside and stuffed two bulging bags into the overhead. They were so big he had to push and shove to get the lid shut.

"Go on," the man said, "sit down."

"Next to the kid? You gotta be kidding. She'll probably throw up or something."

"Come off it, Eunice. She looks harmless enough. Right, kid?" He winked at Birdie.

Birdie turned away. She wasn't getting into that fight. She could hear them going on and on.

He had to have the aisle for his legs. He knew the middle seat was the smallest, and still . . . A voice came over the loudspeaker. Until everyone was seated with their seat belts fastened, the plane could not push back from the gate. With one last *humph*, the woman forced herself into the seat next to Birdie. It was a good thing

Birdie herself was small for her age because the woman's thigh and bottom were all the way under Birdie's side of the armrest.

The woman said a bad word and pushed the armrest up so now she was practically sitting in Birdie's lap. Birdie wasn't going to look at the unhappy couple, and, with her seat belt fastened, she couldn't reach her book or her diary. They were in her backpack under the seat in front of her. So there was nothing for Birdie to do but look out the window at the plane parked next to hers.

She wondered if it was bigger or smaller. She tried to imagine who was sitting right there across from her. Maybe another scared kid. That would be nice. Then she wouldn't feel quite so alone.

She closed her eyes when the plane began to move. *Dear Jesus, don't let the plane crash and kill me.* She meant to keep her eyes closed all the way to Washington, but she couldn't even wait until takeoff. She squinted and watched as they rolled slowly down the field and then stopped. What was the matter? Was something broken? She leaned closer to the window and saw that they were in a line of planes. It would be forever before they even

194

left the ground. So she left her eyes open, watching the stop and go of the planes in the line, wondering where they were all going.

The woman next to her humphed impatiently. "Last time we're taking this airline!" Only she stuck in a cuss word to describe the company.

"Oh, hush," her husband said. He must be her husband, although Daddy never talked to Mom that way.

"I have a bad feeling about this flight," the woman said. "I told you not to take this [another cuss] airline. They're always crashing."

Birdie's heart gave a little lurch.

"Where did you ever get that fool idea?" the man said.

"It was on Facebook," she said. "A lot of people warned against . . ."

"Oh, shaddup! You going to believe every stupid thing you read on social media? I ought to throw away your [cuss word] phone."

"I'll show you!" The woman grabbed her purse out from under her seat. Birdie could see that she'd never turned her phone off. The attendant had told them to turn off "all electronic devices." Sometimes when people didn't turn off their cell phones it interfered with the pilot's whatever. Birdie knew that for a fact, even though she had no idea where she had learned about it. Maybe the humphing woman had put it on airplane mode, but somehow Birdie doubted it.

The woman's elbow was jabbing into Birdie's chest. The huge hand with rings cutting into the flesh of her fingers was shaking as she tried to find a website with the pointer finger of her right hand. See? She'd never put it in airplane mode.

Was the woman shaking because she was scared? Birdie was surprised to see a grown person shaking like that, but that had to be it. The woman was more frightened than Birdie was. Birdie stuck her left hand under her sweater and pressed against her Jesus shirt. Her seatmates were too busy cussing and calling each other names to pay her any attention, so she left her hand there. It was almost like holding hands with Jesus.

The plane made a turn until it was sitting on enormous white stripes painted on the tarmac. The engine roared and then began racing down the runway. With a thrill all the way to her toes, Birdie felt the huge noisy machine lift gently into the air, and then . . . they were flying, really flying. She pressed her nose against the glass. Below lay Lake Champlain, dotted with tiny ice houses and the pickup trucks of the ice fishermen. *You guys better get off that ice!* Didn't they know it was almost April already?

Next came the mountains across into New York and then nothing but clouds, fluffy as cotton balls. Every now and then there was a break in the clouds, and she could see lakes and hills and farmland, some brown, some smeared with patches of snow and miniature houses and barns and silos . . . She couldn't have imagined such a lovely view. She wasn't the least bit scared. She felt close to God this high with all the fleece of clouds and the beautiful world spread out below.

And suddenly she saw something so wonderful, so amazing, so beautiful that she could hardly breathe. The shadow of the plane had fallen on the clouds below, and surrounding the shadow, like a many-colored halo, there glowed a rainbow.

A rainbow was God's promise to Noah that every-thing would be all right. She sat back against the seat.

Her heart was beating fast, not with fear, but with a strange kind of excitement.

When she could no longer feel her heart thumping hard against her chest, she turned toward the window. Once again, she was looking at farms and woodlands and tiny doll-like towns. The shadow on the cloud with its rainbow halo had disappeared. Maybe she had just imagined it. But even if it was just in her mind, she felt warm all over. Like God had sent her a secret message.

16
Fear Not

After she saw, or maybe imagined, the rainbow halo, Birdie found that she was feeling brave, even a bit grown-up, so when the attendant came around, Birdie asked for a Coke. Mom really frowned on kids drinking pop. The attendant didn't hesitate or wonder out loud whether Birdie's parents would approve. She just smiled and stretched across Birdie's two seatmates to hand Birdie a Coke with ice and a tiny bag of pretzels.

The woman asked for gin, and the attendant said she was sorry, but they didn't serve alcohol on these short hops. Then the woman said her favorite cuss word, banged down the armrest, and refused to take anything, even the pretzels.

Now the woman's big left hand was squeezing the armrest, the fingers weighted down by chunky rings. It was rude to stare, but Birdie couldn't help studying the rings. They were all different shapes and sizes. Some were gold and others silver. One had a giant red stone and another a huge green one. Could they possibly be real? Or were they like Alicia's Las Vegas costume—Halloween dress-up jewelry? The hand must have caught her looking because it pulled away, trembling, and went to the woman's mouth.

Although Birdie was feeling happy and brave, she didn't feel brave enough to witness to the woman about Jesus and how he was always telling people to "fear not." She was afraid the woman might say that awful cuss word about Jesus, and Birdie felt a need to protect him from insults.

Jesus was being so kind to her right now, practically holding her hand while they sailed through the air close to heaven. Birdie had seen pictures of the sky, even photos from giant telescopes that showed exploding stars so far away that the fastest spaceships couldn't reach them in anyone's lifetime. God! God made all that.

How could you not believe?

And she'd had a . . . a vision of the plane surrounded by a rainbow. It didn't matter if it was something nobody else could see. She could feel the thrill of her private vision all the way to her little toe. It had made her breathe funny. *It took my breath away.* She'd heard somebody, Mom, maybe, say that once about something. Now she knew what it meant. It did take your breath away—all that wonder.

She ought to say something to the poor woman next to her. She opened her mouth to say something, but before she could form the right words, the woman jabbed her elbow into Birdie's arm as she rooted around in her gigantic purse for something. Finally, she pulled out a brown leather container and unscrewed the top. She took great gulps of something inside.

"How in the hell did you smuggle that on?" her husband yelped, almost knocking the container out of the woman's hand. "Put it away! Now! You don't want to arrive drunk!"

"I need it," she squeaked.

He grabbed it from her. "Gimme the lid!"

She fished into the purse for the lid without luck. She even stroked Birdie's lap as though it might have fallen there. Birdie had trouble not shrinking away from the touch.

The man grabbed the purse off his wife's lap. There was the lid, nestled between the woman's pant legs. He dropped her purse into his own lap, screwed the lid onto the bottle, and put it into his shirt pocket. "There," he said. "Now just settle down so we can all get there in peace."

Birdie thought the woman might fight back, but she didn't. She looked like she was about to cry as she pushed her seat back so far that the man behind her muttered something to his seatmate about blankety-blank selfish passengers.

It didn't seem like a good time to witness out loud, but Birdie was feeling so sorry for the woman that she wanted to do something. Maybe she could write her a note, like one from a secret pen pal. She unfastened her seat belt and slid down enough to stick out her toe and inch her backpack toward her with her foot. Then she pulled it up and felt around until she found a pencil that still had a point. She needed paper, so, reluctantly, she tore a back page out of her precious diary.

Now what to say? She glanced over at her seatmates. The man had replaced the woman's purse and put his seat all the way back. Birdie craned around so she could see them both. The man's eyes weren't quite shut, but he was staring at the ceiling, not at Birdie. There were tears glistening in the woman's squinched-up eyes, and her makeup was streaked down her cheeks. Birdie really did have a mission here. She was sure of it. She licked the point of her pencil and began.

Dear . . . friend? *Friend* hardly seemed the right word. Dear— She gave up and scratched out the ~~Dear~~. Jesus is your friend. That was true because Jesus loved everybody, especially the "least of these," and that awful man had made his wife feel like the very least. Jesus says Fear not. Was that enough? She felt the woman shift. It had to be enough.

Now, where to put the message so the woman would come upon it? It would be great if she could put in into

203

the woman's purse, but the man had shoved it back under the seat where it belonged.

Try as she might, at first she could think of no way to get the purse out and slip the note in it without being caught. And knowing that man, as by now she surely did, he'd be yelling at the attendant to call the police, and how, then, would Birdie explain she was putting something *into* the purse, not taking anything out?

The loudspeaker warned that they would be landing in about twenty minutes, so she had to act quickly, before the couple sat up. She checked to make sure neither of them was looking her way. Then, feeling like a sneak, Birdie undid her seat belt and leaned forward. Whew! The gigantic purse lay open. She stretched until her hand was over the edge of the purse and dropped in the note.

Just in time. The man was bringing his seat forward. Birdie sat back and quickly refastened her belt. She didn't dare look at the man, but she was conscious of his leaning forward and pulling his wife's purse out from under her seat and looking inside. He pulled the gilt fastener over and snapped it shut before putting the purse back in place. Then he punched the woman and told her to sit up.

Thank you, Jesus. Birdie had been a witness. Maybe the woman would read her note and think it was a message from God. She sure needed one.

17
All Shall Be Well

It was beautiful coming down. As beautiful as it was when they'd taken off an hour or so before. Birdie pressed her face against the glass. Way in the distance, she thought she could see a tall white spike glistening in the sunlight. The Washington Monument! But it was gone too quickly to be sure, and they were circling over the crowded buildings of a city that wasn't Washington and then over a river that must be the Potomac. Did George Washington really throw a silver dollar across it? It seemed about as likely as Alicia going to Las Vegas. Poor Alicia. *Please, Jesus, take care of her, wherever she is.*

The woman didn't fasten her seat belt or even bring her seat back to an upright position. The flight attendant had to remind her. After the woman reluctantly obeyed, the attendant leaned across her and spoke to Birdie. "Elizabeth," she said, "please stay seated until everyone else deplanes."

She must have seen the puzzlement and unhappiness on Birdie's face, because she went on in a voice as kind as Mr. Goldberg's. "I'm sorry. It's the rules. I have to make sure there's a responsible person here to meet you."

"Oh. Okay."

The attendant smiled and went on down the aisle checking seat belts, tray tables, and seat backs.

They were flying low over the water. So low that for a few seconds Birdie was worried that there was no land to come down on. But there was. Just in time. The plane landed with hardly a bump, followed by a great rushing noise from the engine, and then, slowly, slowly, they were making their way toward a tower and buildings in the distance. *The Lord is my shepherd. He maketh me to lie down in* . . . It wasn't quite right, but God would know she was grateful to be safely on the earth again, wouldn't He?

Everything in Birdie's body was jiggling. With

207

excitement? With fear? She wasn't sure she could tell the difference anymore. She unfastened her seat belt when the loudspeaker dinged to tell the passengers, all but her, that they could get up and move about the cabin. The man shoved his way into the crowded aisle and stood there, pulling and pushing stuff around in the overhead until he jerked out both gigantic bags. They almost hit another passenger in the head on their way to the floor. The man yanked up the handles.

"C'mon!" he commanded his wife. She grabbed up her purse and put it in the empty seat as she heaved and humphed her way out of the middle seat and into the aisle. The couple ignored the muttering of the people waiting behind them.

They didn't pay any attention to Birdie, either. She hadn't expected them to, but still, she wanted to show that she loved her enemies, even if technically they weren't enemies, so she said, "Have a nice day." She wasn't sure if they could hear her, but it didn't really matter. She had tried.

Finally, the last passenger had passed by her row and gone out of sight, and the attendant came back and took down Birdie's jacket and Gran's suitcase. "Here you go," she said, handing Birdie her jacket. "Thanks for being so patient."

"It's okay. I know you have rules."

The attendant smiled and stepped back so Birdie could slide out of the row, put on her jacket, and sling her backpack over her shoulder. She waited for Birdie to go ahead of her up the aisle and followed, pulling the suitcase. Birdie started to say she could do it herself. She didn't. There might be more rules about that. But she needed for Mom to see that she was fine. "I can pull it now," she said as soon as they were safely off the plane.

The attendant smiled and gave her the handle. "Here you go."

It seemed to be a long way through the twisty sleeve and then through the noisy section where all the sleeves converged. Past all the food and drink stands, out another passageway, at the end of which were signs warning that once you passed them, there was no going back.

But none of that mattered anymore, because there was Mom, standing behind a wheelchair. Birdie could see the brown of his uniform jacket before she could make out the features of his face. A blanket lay over his lap, but she thought she could see where there was a crease instead of a right leg. She bit her lip. She had to be brave. Her stomach churned and her heart thumped as though it was going to burst right out of her chest.

The man in the wheelchair threw open his arms. Birdie dropped the handle of the suitcase, slid her backpack to the floor, and ran right toward those arms. An ugly colored scar slashed across his right cheek, yanking his eye all funny. *Oh, his beautiful face!* Maybe the doctors would fix it before Gran had to see it.

Birdie had tried so hard to be brave, but she couldn't hold back the tears flowing down her cheeks. "Oh, Daddy!"

He grabbed her up in his still-strong arms and lifted her right off her feet. He kissed her, his face already scratchy though it was scarcely three o'clock. Then he turned her and pulled her backward onto his lap. Birdie's left leg was on his left and her right fell into the space where his right leg should have been. He nestled her close and buried his face in her hair. "My precious little Birdie girl," he said. "I've missed you so much." And then he began to cry, too. There was no sound, but she could feel the silent sobs through her back.

She twisted around enough to put a finger on his misshapen face and wipe away the tears she knew were there. "There. There," she said, stroking his bristly cheek. "Shh. Shh. Everything is going to be all right."

18

Love with a Capital Letter

Billy was walking now—running, really. Mom and Daddy had missed his first steps, but Birdie and Gran decided to keep it a secret from them. They would have hated to miss Billy's very first steps. So even though the first time he walked was in late August, they didn't know about it until September. In August Mom was back in DC, visiting with Daddy for his final face surgery.

That day, the day Billy first walked, the three of them, Gran, Birdie, and Billy, were in the kitchen. Gran and Birdie were lingering over their afternoon tea. Well, actually, Birdie's was a glass of milk, but they always called it tea. Billy was sitting on the floor putting blocks into the soup pot and taking them out again. Putting them back in and closing the lid. Opening the lid and taking out each block one by one. Putting them back in one by one . . . you get the picture. Birdie was glad he was busy because she and Gran were able to have a very serious discussion. A "serious theological discussion," Gran called it. Birdie figured that was what you meant when you were having a conversation about God.

Gran started it. "Birdie," she said, "may I ask you a personal question?"

For a minute Birdie thought Gran was about to ask her about girls' growing bodies—that kind of school-nurse personal question, so she hesitated. "I guess," she said finally.

"Do you remember when your father got hurt?"

That was not something Birdie was ever going to forget. "Yes."

"Ever since then, I've been worried about something you said about it being your fault that he was wounded. Remember?"

"Uh-huh."

"You said it was because you hadn't prayed right.

213

I've been puzzled. Where did you get the idea that God had rules about how you should pray? Was that something they talked about at your Bible Camp?"

Birdie tried to think back to last summer. It was just over a year ago, but it seemed like a million years. "I guess so," she said.

"Was it fun? Bible Camp, I mean."

"Mostly," Birdie said. "But it wasn't supposed to be just fun. We had to learn a lot of stuff about God and the Bible."

Gran smiled over the top of her teacup. "And what *stuff* did you learn about God?"

"Well, you know—what the Bible teaches, all that."

"Actually, I'm not sure that I *do* know what the folks at Bible Camp were saying about God and what the Bible teaches." She put down her cup. "I'd love for you to tell me about what you learned."

Birdie watched Billy carefully stowing his blocks and closing the pot lid while she tried to arrange her answer. "Well, it was different, different years. First summer I was only eight. I was so homesick I nearly died."

Gran laughed softly. "I can just imagine."

"But the times I forgot about how homesick I was, I had a pretty good time. We sang all kinds of songs and began to learn Bible verses. Reverend Colston was big on memorizing verses. I liked that because I was really good at memorizing. I even got a prize for doing it best. It was a mustard seed bracelet. My cabinmates were all jealous, but I let them take turns wearing it." She shrugged. "I don't have it anymore. It broke and I lost the little doo-hickey that held the mustard seed." Birdie took a bite out of her brownie and chewed while she remembered. She'd been proud of that bracelet.

"And the next year?" Gran asked. "How was that?"

"Oh, I liked that summer the best. I knew kids from the year before, and Reverend Colston had all these Bible games that would go with the stories so you could remember who did what in the Bible. We had these competitions—sort of like spelling bees. Boys against girls." She grinned. "Girls always won."

Gran laughed. "And last summer? Was that fun, too?"

"Well, it was different."

Gran poured herself another cup of tea and added some milk. The milk was from a proper pitcher. Gran

215

never put the milk carton on the table, not even in the kitchen. "How different?"

"Reverend Colston always taught the little kids, but he had somebody else teach us. I mean, we were the ten-to-twelvers, and he thought we were ready for some real deep Bible study, you know."

Gran just nodded. "And?" She stirred her tea.

"We had this new counselor named Ron. We had to call him Counselor Ron to show our respect. He wasn't a preacher like Reverend Colston, but he was going to be one as soon as he finished college. He was already preaching the Gospel to unbelievers, though, so it was like he was almost a preacher."

Birdie paused so long thinking about that first day with Counselor Ron that Billy stopped playing and looked up as if to see what had caused the sudden quiet. When no one spoke, he dropped the pot lid with a clatter and crawled over to Gran. He grabbed her leg and stag-gered upright, clinging to her leg.

Birdie pressed her lips together and began again. "The first Bible session was about Adam and Eve, and when Counselor Ron read out loud that Adam and Eve were, you know, naked, one of the boys snorted and we all started giggling. Counselor Ron got mad and started yelling because we were making fun of God's Word. Did we want to be saved, he said, or did we want to spend eternity in eternal damnation? He explained how you have to respect God's Holy Word and believe right or you would burn forever in the fires of hell. He only had the one week to save us from the eternal flames, so we better shut up and listen."

"I see," Gran said quietly. "That would certainly have terrified me when I was ten. How—?"

"We sure didn't giggle in Bible study anymore."

"I don't expect you did," Gran said, stroking Billy's hair. "What did he say about God? Did Counselor Ron ever say God loved you?"

"Well, sure. But he didn't want us to think God was like some wishy-washy parent that let his kids get away with murder."

"Or . . . or with believing 'wrong', you mean?"

Birdie wiped her milk mustache off her upper lip. Gran always gave her a cloth napkin, even for tea, so she was careful to use it. "I've been kinda mixed up about that."

"Do you feel like talking about it?" Gran put down her teacup.

"Well . . . well, sure—I mean God loves everybody, but unless . . ." She fingered the edge of her napkin.

"Oh, sweetheart!" Gran reached across the table and put her warm hand on top of Birdie's fidgeting one. "God loves all his children, no matter who they are or what they believe or how they act."

"But if you don't believe right . . ."

"Nobody believes right, Elizabeth. We're none of us smart enough to know how God works or what he thinks. I just look at Jesus, who spent his life with lepers and prostitutes and tax collectors and unbelievers. The people who claimed to have the 'right beliefs' hated Jesus for it. And Jesus loved them anyway. The Gospel says he wept over Jerusalem and prayed for forgiveness for the very people who put him on the cross to die."

Birdie's fingers quieted under Gran's gentle hand. "But if you don't believe in Jesus, you will perish. That means you'll go to hell forever, doesn't it?"

"Elizabeth. Just stop for a minute and use that good mind of yours . . . Now. If you had the same power as

God, can you think of anyone you know whom you would send to hell? Not some terrible murderer or evil dictator . . . someone in your own life who has been cruel or mean to you—would you send them to those everlasting fires Counselor Ron talked about?"

Birdie couldn't speak. That was crazy. Of course she'd never send anyone she loved or even liked a tiny bit into the flames of hell forever. No matter what they believed or what they did. What about Wayne or Devon? No, not for five minutes, as much as she had hated them last year. Certainly not poor lying Alicia or her horrible crazy mother . . . She shook her head.

"No one?"

Birdie shook her head again.

"So if you wouldn't want anyone you know, even someone you really dislike, to go to hell, how could you imagine that God, who knows every heart and loves every life—how could we possibly imagine that God, who is Love with a capital L, would send even one of the children he has made and cherished to eternal punishment?"

"But the Bible says . . ."

"Elizabeth, do you know anywhere in the Bible where it says that you or I are more loving than God?"

Birdie shook her head slowly. That wouldn't make any sense. God surely had to be kinder than she was. "So—you believe God loves everyone no matter what?"

"With all my heart," Gran said.

At that moment, like a sign from heaven, William Alexander Cunningham, aged one year, one month, and twelve days, let go of Gran's leg and took three wobbly steps toward his sister. Birdie grabbed him just before his little round bottom hit the linoleum.

"He walked!" Birdie yelled. "Did you see, Gran? Billy walked!"

"He certainly did! At least three steps!" They burst into laughter.

Billy, still in Birdie's firm grasp, looked up at his sister in puzzlement and then over to the face of his beloved Gran. And decided, no matter the reason, to clap his hands and join his baby crowing to the sound of their joy.

Birdie opened the drawer of the small bureau and took out her **I ❤ JESUS** T-shirt. She hadn't worn it for months, but, somehow, she wanted to today. The old dinginess had been scrubbed away, leaving only a faint trace of pink. Gran had suggested she put it in the dryer, so now, when she pulled it on, it felt soft against her skin. She patted the faded heart. "Daddy is coming home today," she whispered. "Home for good."

Daddy had been home for short visits, but today he was coming home to stay. His face was almost back to the way she had always known it, and he was walking really well on his new leg. "I'll be on the ski slopes by next winter," he had bragged, but Birdie didn't care if he never skied again. Skiing could be dangerous, and she just wanted him to stay safe.

Mom had gone to Washington to help him get ready to leave the hospital—he could continue his PT closer to home from now on. As Birdie finished dressing, she felt a pinch of longing for her green sweater. She had felt almost beautiful in that sweater, no matter what Alicia had said. But God loved all His lost and lonely children, like Gran said, so surely His heart had reached out to Alicia. Maybe He had wanted her to have something especially nice, like Birdie's favorite sweater.

She and Gran decided they should take Billy with them to the airport. It would be easier to leave him with Mrs. Shelton. Still, even with all the hassle of the stroller, all three of them should be there to celebrate.

"But Elizabeth, no matter how much he carries on, begging to get down, do *not* let me weaken. We simply cannot be chasing him all over the airport."

Birdie buckled Billy into his front-facing big-boy car seat while Gran folded the bulky stroller and wrestled it into the trunk of the Subaru. "I shouldn't suggest this, Elizabeth, but would you sit up front? I can't drive safely if I'm always craning my neck around to talk with you."

Birdie loved talking with Gran. She got in and buckled up.

It was one of those bright, clear late-winter mornings after a fresh snow, when the sky is so blue and the earth so white that you are filled with the wonder of creation. As they drove, Birdie thought of her flight to Washington so long ago when, looking out the airplane window, her eyes had been dazzled by the rainbow halo on the clouds.

"Gran, did I ever tell you about this amazing thing I saw the first time I flew to Washington to see Daddy?"

"No, I don't think so. What thing?"

Gran clicked the signal to pass an out-of-state driver who seemed to be staring out his window at the snow on Mount Hunger as he poked along at forty-five miles per hour. Birdie waited. You are never supposed to distract a driver. As she watched Gran skillfully make the maneuver, she suddenly realized that she had been wrong.

Gran wasn't plain or even just pretty when she smiled. Gran was beautiful. Not the kind of beautiful Mom was, but her own Gran kind of beautiful.

"You were about to say?" Gran said when they were safely past and in the proper lane.

"Well, you may not remember, but I was sort of nervous about that trip . . ." She waited for Gran to say something like *Of course I remember*, but Gran didn't comment, so Birdie continued. "It was a wonderful day—just like today. We were really high up over the clouds. I looked out the window, and I could see the shadow of the plane on the clouds. But it wasn't just a regular shadow. I mean, around the shadow was this kind of rainbow, like a halo. It was so gorgeous, it just took my breath away." She stopped to take a deep breath before she went on. "After it disappeared, I thought maybe it had just been my imagination . . ."

"Oh, no, Elizabeth. It wasn't your imagination." Gran glanced over at Birdie, who saw excitement written all over her grandmother's lovely face. "That is *so* wonderful!" Gran said. "You saw a glory."

"A what?" Birdie thought she'd heard wrong.

"A glory. That's what scientists call that iridescent phenomenon you saw. It's one of the most beautiful sights in the heavens."

"Gran! In the Bible when people see a glory, they know that God is, well, it's like God is right there, showing himself to them. Do—do scientists know that?"

"I should think so," Gran said. "Why else would they call it a glory?"

Acknowledgments

After I finish a book, I say to myself, *Well, that was a good career while it lasted,* because I'm convinced that every book will be my last. My family long ago stopped paying any attention to my whine, and I stopped saying it aloud even though I still think so. When you reach your eighties, however, the notion has to be taken seriously. I am, therefore, particularly grateful for the people and circumstances that made it possible for this book to be written and published.

In the summer of 2018, I had the joy of becoming a quasi-student of the Vermont College of Fine Arts, where I have been a member of the board of trustees since its inception.

I went with a group of faculty and students for a

summer residency in Bath, England. There, in a workshop led by David Gill, I managed to put together two disparate ideas that had lounged around aimlessly for years in my disorganized brain. I am very grateful to the Pickwick Plotters, along with their faculty members David Gill and Varian Johnson and program director Lori Steel. Especial thanks to Cathy Petter, who picked up a number of my Post-it story elements from the floor and shared her excellent notes.

It was either cold feet or a busy fall schedule that kept me from actually starting to work, but a fortuitous event occurred on Valentine's Day 2019. I slipped on a patch of ice and broke both my left ankle and leg. All four of my children took turns caring for their crippled parent, but my sons thought broken bones a poor excuse for laziness. John bought me a new table the right height for my wheelchair, and David gave me a set of barbells to strengthen my arms so I could more easily wheel myself there. I am grateful to Lin and Mary for their loving concern and their brothers for making sure I would not waste any time during my convalescence.

No thanks are adequate for the skill, energy, and

enthusiasm of my amazing agent, Susie Cohen, and for Karen Lotz, publisher extraordinaire, who still took the time and effort to edit my work in the midst of an impossible schedule further scrambled upon the advent of COVID-19. To all the crew at Candlewick who show such care in the making of books for children and young people: Please know how much I appreciate you all, especially Olivia Swomley, who has fought with alien processing programs on my behalf and won. Thank you for your know-how and your infinite patience. And to Maya Myers, who had the burden of rearranging my commas and challenging me when it mattered, my sometimes grumpy gratitude.

I am eternally grateful to Nancy Graff, who, since my husband's death, is my first reader as well as my cherished friend. And I guess I have to thank my ten-year-old self, who has continued to hang around and inspire, although she was so often a colossal pain when I first knew her.

And, finally, thanks to Sister Ann Duhaime, with her transforming question: "Where have you seen God lately?"